Reviews of REMARKABLE

"For the several hours while I read REMARKABLE, I felt I walked in the shoes of Stanley James McMillen. It is a very human document."

---- Bernard Rink, Masters of Library Science,
Collegiate Liberian, emeritus

"A tale of Stanley McMillen and the patients he cared for, and his friends, all with lives and stories that unfolded…one page at a time. The characters hold true to who they are. The reader will fall in love with their personalities. I felt like the intermission curtains would come down between chapters if this was a movie!"

---- Crystal Lynn Warren, BSN,
Critical Care Specialist

"REMARKABLE is a book of relationships - honest and gripping, it connects to readers through raw emotion. While I was reading, I found myself reflecting on my own life, and felt I knew the characters. And I truly loved the dog."

----Diane Lundin, MS, Resolution Book Club

"This Remarkable story takes place in the city of Big Bay within the settings of a high paced, critical care unit of the hospital and amongst the countless hours of humanized relationships intermingled between nurses and the patrons of Poor Joe's Tavern. A must read novel that intertwines the real life raw emotions and relationships between inconspicuous life-long friends. It is a 'Remarkable' must read journey."

---- Wendy Murton-Helmka, MS, PT Retired

Remarkable

a Novel

Richard Alan Hall

Dreams are only ideas unless we believe

Richard Alan Hall

rahBOOKs
keep it under your hat publisher

This is a work of fiction. There are some people that actually exist who appear in this novel. The singer and songwriter Miriam Pico, and the composer musician David Chown actually live in Traverse City, Michigan. They perform in Northern Michigan and Key West. I am grateful for their permission to be part of this story. Thank you also to Glen Lundin, who owns Rolling Hills Antiques in Traverse City, and Jillena Avery Kellogg R.N., who always wanted to be a Hospice Nurse. The remaining cast of characters you are about to meet I discovered as they traveled through my mind and are fictitious, as are the City of Big Bay, Big Bay General Hospital and Poor Joe's Bar. Any similarity to real persons, living or dead, as well as places and events, is coincidental. I hope you grow to love these characters as much as I have.

Second Edition, August 2013

Printed in the United States of America

To contact the author, email: rahall49684@gmail.com
Visit the author's facebook page at: Richard Alan Hall – Author

To order additional copies of REMARKABLE visit:
http://lulu.com/spotlight/RichardAlanHall
Or call: 1-800- 587-2147

rahBOOKs
keep it under your hat publisher

To Debra Jean Hall

Wisdom is knowing the right thing to do. Courage is doing the right thing regardless of consequences. What a remarkable combination, this stuff of heroes.

Richard Alan Hall

ACKNOWLEDGEMENTS

Thank you to Dr. William Smith for our weekly walks along West Bay where I bounced ideas off him. I also thank Bernie Rink, Jim Rink, Nancy Vogl, Anne Marie Kucera, Crystal Lynn Warren, Wendy Helmka, Diane Lundin and Jillena Kellogg for their ideas and suggestions.

Thank you to artist Janet Chown for creating REMARKABLE's cover.

Thank you to my editor Lisa Mottola Hudon. She did the hard work. (www.lisamottolahudon.com)

Most of all, I thank Debra J. Hall, my wife. It is because of her love and chronic insistence that this novel was written.

And thanks to our Eternal Daddy for the inspirations that made this possible.

TABLE OF CONTENTS

REMARKABLE

PROLOGUE

S tanley James McMillen loved to be unpredictable; it created a certain level of excitement in his life. He certainly did not fit the image of a registered nurse in the 1970's.

He had been the starting quarterback for the high school football team. During his college years he joined a Golden Gloves boxing club, and eventually went on to become the State Light Heavyweight Champion.

Stanley was six feet tall with dark curly hair just long enough to cover his ears. Nearsighted, he wore horn-rimmed glasses that made him look like a cross between a Rhodes Scholar and a midday television soap opera star.

Electrical Engineering was his initial course of study. He found it boring. One night, Stanley read an article in a men's magazine about men studying to become registered nurses and the idea fascinated him for no particular reason other than it was "way different," and he did not know any men who were nurses.

The Saturday night pool players' consortium had gathered at Poor

Joe's Tavern for the weekly rituals of beer consumption, political analysis, girl watching and general announcements.

"I've changed my major," Stanley announced to the assembled jury. "I'm going into nursing; I'm going to be a registered nurse."

Complete silence in Poor Joe's.

"Are you switching teams?" asked a newcomer to the consortium.

Stanley slowly turned his head and looked at the fellow as those around the newcomer backed away as if he was contagious.

"You really want to go there?" Stanley asked the unfortunate as he pointed towards the front door.

"Sorry man....sorry…just a joke……bad joke…sorry."

The banter resumed and Stanley humbly took the anticipated grief on his decision for several hours.

"Well boys, have to go…just remember, nursing is where the ladies are. Call me when you get desperate." And with that, Stanley walked out of Poor Joe's and into a cool September night. *This is going to be fun,* he thought to himself.

* * *

Dr. Garrison Skinner was the most feared professor on the entire campus. He entered the lecture hall that first morning clutching several books and a mass of loose papers under his left arm while trying to relight his pipe using his right hand. He marched down the steps to the lectern without looking left or right.

Every eye in the auditorium was fixed on him as he made the first proclamation, "Do not become good friends with the persons sitting on either side of you as they will not likely be here next term.

"Welcome to Anatomy and Physiology. Hello to nursing, a noble profession which is known to devour its young," he continued as he wiped tobacco ashes from the lectern.

Little did Stanley realize that he was being launched into a career that would occur during the most exciting period in modern medicine, and that he would experience a kaleidoscope of events exhibiting the remarkable human spirit which endures even in the face of terror and tragedy because of loyalty and love.

Chapter 1

A Painful Itch

T he hospital night shift, staffed with World War II and Korean War nurses wearing starched white uniforms, made swishing sounds as they moved about the third floor nursing station. Even their nursing hats were starched. Stanley rubbed his sweaty palms together and felt a throbbing in his throat as he walked into the nurses' station for his first night as a Registered Nurse. His mouth felt dry and he had no spit to swallow.

A serious nursing shortage resulted in little time spent orienting new nurses, the emphasis being placed on filling the staffing roster and then learning the "lay of the land" as things progressed.

The air felt sticky and the gentle breeze from the south smelled of pine needles that hot August night in a hospital without air conditioning. The nursing station, dimly lit and with blue cigarette smoke extending from the ceiling halfway to the floor, had white walls. On the gold and black speckled gray tile floor sat a large white metal foot tub filled with ice cubes being fanned by a brass oscillating GE fan that made a click-clicking sound as the blades hit its protective guard. Ash trays, strategically placed by the telephones and in the medication room, were half filled with spent butts, mostly Salem and Camels.

"Chief" was in charge. Having served in Europe and witness to the worst that war had to offer, she seemed unintimidated by anything known to man. No one questioned Chief, even the Doctors deferred to her.

And there she sat, next to the phone and the ice-filled metal foot tub in a smoke-filled nurses' station with a Camel cigarette hanging from the left side of her mouth. She looked small in comparison to the other nurses. Her long auburn hair, with shiny little treads of silver, was neatly pulled back in a French twist. Bobby pins strategically placed, kept stray wisps in place. She looked at Stanley over the rim of her tortoise shell reading glasses and asked, "Well, are you the Stanley McMillen we've all heard about?" as she looked him up and down several times.

She inhaled deeply and continued, "You can call me Chief...and this is Cap over here and you will meet Nancy and the others later. You sure do look young, but don't worry; we will teach you more than you ever learned in college."

About 3am, a local ambulance pulled up to the Emergency Room door. The driver pushed the red button at the entrance to the ER, alerting the staff that he had a patient. (The ER was staffed by the floor nurses at night during those early years). With the examination completed, the patient rode in a squeaky wheelchair to be admitted with the diagnosis of "acute urinary retention."

"Time for you to get some work done; go cath him, but don't take off more than 1000 cc's or he might go into shock." It was Stan's first patient care order from Chief.

"Hi, my name is Stanley. What's your name sir?" Stanley asked.

"They call me Arthur... they do."

"I hear you are having a peeing problem Arthur."

"I hain't had a decent piss in a week."

"Really!"

"And I got a painful itch down there." Arthur pointed to his groin.

Arthur lived a humble existence. He had obviously not bathed in recent history, and still had on his winter underwear, gray and soiled. He also had several layers of clothing over the long-johns. The filthy layers smelled of urine and an odor reminiscent of rotten chicken. After removing the clothing and getting Arthur into bed, Stanley prepped him and prepared to insert a urinary catheter.

"You look three months pregnant Arthur."

Arthur had not been circumcised. As Stanley retracted the foreskin, he saw movement, and as he retracted his foreskin further, several maggots fell out and wiggled on the sterile drape.

Now, Stanley was a farm boy. He had grown up on a farm and thought that there was no smell or circumstance that would bother him.

He was wrong.

Stunned, Stanley walked down the hall back to the nurses' station where Chief and Cap were setting up the morning medications. They both turned and looked as he walked in, still wearing rubber gloves.

"Maggots…he has maggots under his foreskin."

"How much urine you get back?" was Chief's only response.

"I didn't get that far yet."

"Well you be sure and clamp it off at 1000 cc's. I bet he has 2 liters in him."

Chief and the gloved Stanley walked back to the patient's room together.

"Yup, maggots…they won't bite you." And she was gone.

"Ouch…ouch…..damn you….," Arthur yelled as Stanley pushed the catheter into his urethra.

"Almost there Arthur, hang on…." And the catheter passed a swollen prostate and into the bladder.

Bloody urine gushed into the collection bag.

"How long you been peeing blood Arthur?"

"Long time."

"Ever mention this to a doctor?"

"None of their business."

Stanley clamped the catheter after 1000 cc's were drained. An hour later another 1000 cc's flowed into the collection bag.

The sun had just peeked over the east hills of Big Bay when Arthur announced to Stanley, "Arthur wants to go now."

"Arthur, we need to get you a new set of clothes before you leave. Somebody will go down to the Salvation Army and get you new clothes, ok?"

"OK."

All totaled, Arthur had 2500 cc's (2.6 quarts) of urine stored in his bladder.

That morning Cap showed Stanley the morning cleansing routine.

Per Chief's instructions, all of the "stainless" in the nurses' station, utility room and kitchen area must be cleaned using rubbing alcohol and a cotton towel. No one was to use any of these areas after the cleansing. If any sink or counter-top had to be used, the cleansing must be repeated before the day shift appeared at 7am. No exceptions. And the ash trays were to be emptied and put away in the bottom drawer in the medication room.

It might have been the rubbing alcohol or perhaps the maggot experience; Stanley felt dizzy while driving his Volkswagen towards home that morning.

Arthur signed himself out of the hospital two days later. The hospital did provide him with a clean pair of pants and a nice summer shirt.

Chapter 2

Wendell Joins the Bait

W endell, the night custodian, had keys to the hospital kitchen and therefore was considered an indispensable member of the night shift.

In these years, there were no cafeteria services for the night shift, leaving the options of a cold lunch from home or Wendell securing delectable tidbits from the walk-in refrigerators around 2am.

Wendell was held in high esteem.

He stood five feet, eleven inches. His curly brown hair had a little gray at the temples. His brown eyes always seemed to have a twinkle with a hint of pain. He looked fit, except for a slight limp and a disfigured right hand, consisting of only a thumb and forefinger.

The night shift suited his lifestyle perfectly, especially in the winter. Wendell loved ice fishing. He took great pride in consistently being the first person each year to go out on the ice of Big Bay and chop a hole.

It had been a colder than usual December and skim ice had formed on the Bay. Wendell excitedly approached as Stanley walked through the

ER entrance on his way to the time clock.

"You want to go fishing with me in the morning?" Wendell asked.

"Wendell, are you nuts? The bay just froze over yesterday," Stanley replied with a grin on his face.

"I got a system," Wendell answered. "I go one step at a time and pound the spud in front of me and when the spud goes through the ice, I stop right there and spud a hole and start fishing."

"I got the sleigh all stocked up and ready to go," he continued, referring to a wooden sled he had adapted to carry one case of Drewrys beer (long neck bottles), an assortment of bait, extra fishing line and a compartment to store extra cigarettes.

"Well I'm going to pass on this one trip Wendell. Good luck out there. I hope you catch your limit."

Wendell and his spud went through the ice at the same instant that morning. With great fanfare, the volunteer fire department formed a human chain. The final man in the chain was able to wiggle on the pulsating ice close to the hole, reach into the frigid water and grab Wendell as he bobbed around among the contents of his sled. Semiconscious and suffering from hypothermia and exposure, Wendell spent eleven days in the hospital. He repeated the story to Stanley and anyone else who would listen every night.

"I was making good headway out from the power plant," Wendell said. "There was a good two inches or so of ice. And then I hit the ice with my spud one more time and all the ice around me collapsed and down I went, spud and sled and all. Last thing I remember before they pulled me out was a pack of Marlboros bobbing in front of me…. hit me in the nose."

The hospital's food service director noted that the employees' cafeteria food costs dropped while Wendell was hospitalized.

Wendell continued that crazy ice fishing tradition for many more years. He never fell through the ice again.

"I don't think I could go back on the ice after a close call like that," Stanley mentioned to Wendell one morning as they sipped coffee in the hospital cafeteria.

"I've been through worse," Wendell said, looking directly into

Stanley's eyes, and then he laughed.

Chapter 3

No One Said There Would Be Nights Like This

F or the first six months Stanley often felt sick to his stomach as he walked around in a sleep deprived haze. He worked the 11pm to 7am shift five days a week while attending classes each Tuesday, Wednesday, and Thursday from 1pm to 3pm. The classes were taught by Dr. C.C. Earl, a Cardiologist from Flint, Michigan.

In the 1950's and 60's as well as the early 1970's, the chances of dying from a heart attack were in the neighborhood of 1 in 3. Then a precedent setting nursing unit opened at the Presbyterian-University Medical Center. They established an Intensive Coronary Care Unit staffed by nurses educated in acute intervention who had been granted the authority to treat life threatening arrhythmias and the other complications associated with heart attacks. Soon word spread across the nation that hundreds of lives were being saved each year. By the mid 1970's all hospitals of consequence had plans to open a Coronary Care Unit.

Dr. Earl had accepted the request from the medical staff and a close friend to teach and conduct a preceptor program for a select group of enthusiastic nurses to staff a Coronary Care Unit. Stanley was chosen to be part of this very first class and it changed everything in his nursing career.

Following 6 months of classes and weekly tests and then the mother of all final exams (actually more difficult than State Boards, Stanley thought), Big Bay General had a specialized nursing staff ready to staff a Coronary Care Unit.

While the actual CCU was being constructed (an 8 bed unit and a 14 bed step down unit), a one bed unit opened in room 314 directly across from the nurses' station. That room, fully equipped with heart monitoring equipment, automatic rotating tourniquets, a ventilator, oxygen tent and a defibrillator, became the very first Coronary Care Unit in the state.

Stanley's mind raced from treatment algorithm to algorithm as he drove to work for the first night in the new unit. He listened to an 8 track tape, "Shades of Time," by the Pozo Seco Singers, as he went over the new treatment options in his mind. Stanley could hear the beep…beep…beeping of the cardiac monitor coming from room 314 as he walked off the elevator. "You got a patient in the CCU," Wendell announced proudly. Cap pointed towards the room from the nurses' station and gave a thumbs up signal.

The patient arrived earlier that morning, suffering from an anterior wall myocardial infarction. He lived in a rental mobile home. An acquaintance of the patient told Dr. Earl about a history of considerable alcohol consumption, although the patient stated on admission, "I ain't had no drinks for a couple of days cuz I'm flat broke right now."

Wendell completed the 2am grocery delivery and everyone finished eating. Chief had the night off, leaving Cap, Nancy and Stanley to staff the CCU and 3rd floor. Nancy was sitting in the CCU while Stanley answered a patient call light at the other end of the hall.

Suddenly things unfolded like a cheap late night horror movie.

On the third floor came a chilling scream that no one present would ever forget.

"He's killing me…. HELP… HELP…. Stanley…. HELP…. Oh

HELP ME!"

And then the tinkling sound of glass breaking and equipment crashing and more screams and then sobbing.

And then a dull THUD sound.

Stanley sprinted the length of the hall to room 314. He found Nancy lying on the floor curled up and covering her head with her arms as a crazed naked man continually kicked her with his bloody bare feet. Little puddles of blood splattered the gray tile floor, bridged by chaotic bloody footprints. Long lines of blood extended up the white walls and cascaded across the ceiling. Dark venous blood flowed freely from the severed intravenous line that the patient had torn apart. Blood oozed from Nancy's mouth and nose. She had a jagged laceration on her forehead, and blood was flowing into her left eye. Stanley charged the man and pushed him away from Nancy. The patient fell on the bed. Grabbing Nancy by her left ankle, Stanley started to pull her towards the door when she screamed "DUCK STANLEY!" just as the patient swung a bed-mounted IV pole at Stanley's head like a lethal weapon. The years of trained boxing reflexes saved him in that instant, as the tip of the pole grazed Stanley's forehead just as his head snapped backwards. Stanley picked up a bedside chair and hurled it at the crazy man, knocking the patient to the floor. While glaring intently at the prone man, he carefully dragged Nancy the rest of the way out of the room just as Wendell arrived and pulled the door shut, trapping the patient inside.

"You want me to go in there with you and tackle him?" Wendell asked rather calmly.

"Let's wait for help Wendell; he's out of his mind," Stanley replied.

Cap had already called Dr. Earl, who had in turn called the police for help, and all arrived within 10 minutes. Wendell held the door to 314 tightly shut. All the while, the patient tried repeatedly to break the windows of his third floor room using the bedside commode (which he had recently used, just making the scene even more bazaar). He was cursing and screaming, "You bastards think of everything…break-proof glass…damn you!"

A sheriff's deputy counted, "One…two….three……" and Wendell

opened the door. Two city cops, one sheriff's deputy, Dr. Earl, Wendell and Stanley charged into a hail of flying objects, including a metal bedpan, a glass IV bottle, a partially filled metal urinal and various rarely heard obscenities. Together they tackled the man to the bloody floor. Dr. Earl gave the struggling patient a dose of Sodium Pentothal and shortly thereafter a sleeping patient was lifted back into bed and secured with leather restraints.

"I haven't seen anything like that since I was an intern at Bellevue!" exclaimed Dr. Earl. "Is everyone alright?"

"Nancy is hurt," Cap replied. "She should go to the ER"

Dr. Earl personally took Nancy to the ER in a wheelchair.

Nancy had several fractured ribs, a one inch laceration above her left eye and a broken nose.

"I should have been the one in the room with that nut," Stanley said to Cap after the police left the building. "Damn it!"

The patient survived this heart attack and the Delirium Tremors.

Nancy missed work for six weeks. That attack hurt her deeply. The pain that someone would do such a thing to her never went away.

Chapter 4

Pride in Passing

T he new eight bed Coronary Care Unit opened on a warm summer day. A large white tent was erected on the hospital lawn to accommodate many dignitaries and Big Bay citizens as well as the local radio and television news services. Even a U.S. Senator arrived in time for the ribbon cutting. The whole proceeding could have easily been confused for a carnival.

And then the shiny new Big Bay General Coronary Care Unit opened. The occasion seemed even more exciting for Stanley as he had been promoted to the assistant unit manager.

In retrospect, those were the Model T days of Critical Care. They used oxygen tents and rotating tourniquets. Every patient received an IV solution of "Polarizing Solution." Bed rest was absolute for the first 3 days, and then patients would be allowed to feed themselves a full liquid diet; this regime all made bearable for the patients by around-the-clock sedation. Total hospitalization following a heart attack commonly lasted three weeks.

But it worked. And it worked because of the nursing staff's ability to intervene and treat life threatening conditions that previously had resulted in death.

The survival rate for acute myocardial infarction patients improved from a previous 66 percent to 75 percent that first year, and then to 80 percent by 1980. It would not be until the advent of Interventional Cardiology, decades later, that the survival rate would increase to 90 percent.

Numbers are just figures without faces. The faces being treated had lives and fears and stories and families who loved them.

* * *

Her name was Panika and she was the Matriarch of the Chippewa Indians. Panika was dying. Admitted following a massive anterior wall myocardial infarction while at home, she had now developed pulmonary edema and was struggling for each breath under the oxygen tent.

Soon after her admission, a young man approached Stanley and introduced himself as her grandson and humbly asked permission for him and three brothers to "take turns staying with her," while pointing towards bed number two. Stanley had no idea what he was agreeing to.

The four grandsons rotated a sentinel position at the foot of her bed on an hourly basis around the clock. Never in the way, and never spoke unless spoken to, these four young men became Stanley's favorite "guards." He admired their devotion.

The grandsons standing at the foot of the Matriarch's bed were obviously not considered by the family as part of the two visitors per patient limitation. Around the clock, two other family members would be in attendance at the bedside, usually just quietly holding her hand through a small opening in the oxygen tent. At times, soft conversations would take place. On occasion, gentle laughter could be heard coming from both inside and outside the oxygen tent.

The family never left her bedside, except when requested.

"Why are they so special?" a raspy cigarette voice asked from behind Stanley as he stood in the medication room. "Heard they been here all night and don't keep to the visiting hours like the rest of us do."

Stanley felt the hair on his neck stand up and his jaw tightened. *You have got to be kidding,* he was thinking to himself as he turned to see a weathered looking elderly lady with unwashed gray hair held in place with bobby pins, pointing towards bed two.

"I'm sorry, I don't quite understand. Are they bothering you?"

"Nope, but rules be rules," she retorted.

"Our visiting hours actually are designed for the recovery of our patients. There are occasions like this when it is best for the patient to have extended visitation time and to spend time with the people who have mattered to them all their life."

"If you would like to spend more time with your uncle let us know and we'll work it out for you," Stanley continued.

The lady gave Stanley a sardonic glare and left the unit without saying another word.

Within 24 hours the word had spread throughout the Native American community. Tents popped up on the hospital lawn next to the apple trees. Panika's extended family now maintained vigilance next to her on the hospital lawn--a small city of Native American families living in tents, in station wagons and in sleeping bags spread on the lawn. The new village occupied an acre. Frequently the extended family gathered on the lawn by some ancient apple trees and they seemed to be praying together.

Stanley was working inside Panika's oxygen tent changing IV bottles when she looked over his left shoulder. Her eyes widened and she exclaimed, "Oh! My abinoojiiyens! She is here!"

Standing between the sentinel grandsons at the foot of the bed was a small slender beautiful young lady smiling and waving at her grandmother. She looked like a youthful version of Panika. Her brilliant brown eyes sparkled with tears that left tracks as they trickled down her cheeks. Her long black hair was in two braids, extending from her shoulders and resting on each breast.

"That's my granddaughter from New York City; I am very happy now...minawaaigozi!"

Stanley stepped back while the granddaughter poked her head into the oxygen tent, kissing her grandmother on the forehead, dripping tears and draping braids on her grandmother's face.

"Thank you ...thank you ...thank you for coming all this way. Thank you Gichi-manidoo for getting her to me safely.....Everything is just fine my precious one.......we are never far apart are we?"

Their faces touched as they gently rocked back and forth together, sobbing.

Stanley took several deep breaths, biting his bottom lip until it bled, attempting to prevent tears. It did not work. A grandson moved towards Stanley and gently put both arms around him, and whispered in Stanley's right ear, "They have been one spirit for as long as I can remember...much zaagi (love)."

Panika lived for 3 more days. The day she died she grasped Stanley's hand and pulled him close to her face and whispered, "A person cannot become a human being until their mirrors become windows."

When she died, four Tribal Elders wrapped her in a ceremonial blanket. Then the four grandsons entered her room and carried her down the hallway past wide-eyed staff to the elevator and out of the hospital. As the staff watched from the 3rd floor windows, the grandsons carried their Matriarch down the hospital driveway lined on either side by family members. The young men held their chins high in the air as they carried her while their chests were sobbing.

The grandsons and elders gently placed her in the back of a Ford station wagon. Then they helped the granddaughter climb in beside her beloved grandmother. She lay with her left arm over the blanket, hugging the dearest person she had ever known.

I have never felt such a powerful love, Stanley thought as he watched the procession turn left and drive north. And he wiped his eyes using the back of his hands.

Chapter 5

Ciao, The Miracle Boy

T he family of migrant farm workers drove north across the
border from Juarez, Mexico hoping to find work picking
asparagus, strawberries and other row crops. The weeklong trip had been
plagued by mechanical problems with their rickety green 1948 REO truck.
The wooden flatbed with three wooden benches secured, had a canvas top
stretched from the eight foot tall wooden railings, and it made a flapping
sound in the wind as the truck traveled down the highways. There was a big
sense of relief when they arrived at the farm, especially since the last 200
miles were driven with the right front tire showing an ever growing bulge
that had made a cloppity-clop sound as they drove.

Ciao, a spirited seven year old boy with thick black hair and
sparkling brown eyes, laughed as he pushed his big sister in a tire swing
suspended from the limb of a great oak tree 20 feet from the parked REO
truck. His father and uncle struggled to remove the truck tire from the rim.
It was a split rim tire, common on large trucks, and split rims can be dan-

gerous.

The two men grunted and strained. The old tire and rim seemed fused as one. Suddenly the split rim separated like a giant spring and a portion of it boomeranged through the air.

The flying metal struck the young boy just below the left knee and severed his leg through the bone, leaving the lower portion of his leg connected only by a flap of skin.

With panic and horror, young Ciao screamed in pain and then quickly slumbered into unconsciousness. Bright blood spurted from his amputated leg. The farmer ran from the barn with his car keys in his hand. Ciao's nearly severed leg flopped about awkwardly while being carried by his terrified farther, who climbed into the back seat of the farmer's Rambler sedan. The farmer pushed the gas pedal to the floor and gravel spit up from the rear tires. The black car sped south on the Nine Hills Highway towards the hospital. Even at speeds of 80 miles per hour, the drive to the hospital took 20 minutes.

Stanley was in the ER admitting a cardiac patient when Ciao's father ran through the door carrying his pale, limp son. The little boy's left leg hung at a gruesome angle, swinging back and forth. Both father and son were covered with dark congealed blood.

The man's face, smeared with his son's blood, was a portrait of terror and pain. Wide eyed, his dark pupils were dilated with fear. His tears made little tracks through the dried blood on his left cheek. His lips trembled.

Ciao's uncle had taken a belt and tightened it above the knee, but it was obvious that there had been a significant amount of blood lost.

"Ayude a mi hijo....Help! Please...help us!" The father screamed in broken English. And with that, he placed the bloody unconscious boy in Stanley's arms.

The ER crew and the surgeon who had been summoned from the OR worked quietly and quickly to establish several IV sites and to stop the arterial bleeding that resumed when the child was given blood transfusions and IV fluids.

Richard Alan Hall

A pickup truck driven by the distraught uncle pulled up to the ER entrance with the young boy's mother and older sister.

Ciao's mother could speak no English and her husband very little. There was no one on duty in the hospital who could understand Spanish. The distraught mother hugged Stanley, sobbing, pulling at his bloody white lab coat, crying and mourning in Spanish, "Por favor Senor, salve a mi hijo! El es un nino precioso, por favor salvelo. Mi corazon esta rompiendose!" A giant of a man with tear tracks through the dried blood of his son stood in the middle of the ER, limp arms hanging by his side, both hands dark with dried blood. A beautiful young Mexican girl wearing a green summer dress with a large blood stain on the left hip that had happened when she picked her writhing little brother off the ground, now stood next to her daddy with a blank stare of shock in her eyes. A farmer wearing blood stained bib overalls paced, as did the uncle. And nearby in the nurses' station, gathered the Emergency Room staff with the heaviness in their hearts which occurs with each accident that involves children. This is the picture that would remain in the minds of each person involved in the Big Bay ER that morning, forever.

Ciao's sister's name was Maria. At age 13, she easily passed for 17 and provided a great temptation for many a young man until her giant father was spotted. Maria loved to read, and had taught herself both English and some French while riding in the back of the REO truck as her parents drove from work site to work site around Mexico and the United States.

"I speak English," she said as she walked towards Stanley.

The surgeon had no optimism as he left for the operating room.

"The boy has lost an awful lot of blood, been in shock for at least 30 minutes and we have no blood pressure. Let's move!"

The Coronary Care Unit actually served as an Intensive Care Unit as well. The staff prepared to recover and care for this young boy when he came out of the operating room.

Stanley took the mother, father, sister, uncle and farmer to the CCU waiting room.

Ninety minutes later, a very pale 7 year old's stretcher wheeled past the waiting room and into unit bed four.

With terror and deep sadness in their brown tear-reddened eyes, the family entered Ciao's room. The little boy that they loved lay unconscious in a bed. He was as pale as the sheets wrapped around him. Suspended above him, hanging from several IV poles, were blood, plasma, and saline solutions running to IV sites in both arms and a subclavian central line. The cardiac monitor showed a sinus tachycardia with a heart rate in the 130's.

For the next 48 hours Ciao remained unconscious. That was not an encouraging sign. The only good news: his kidneys seemed to be functioning despite the prolonged lack of blood pressure, and the below the knee amputation showed no signs of serious infection.

His mother and sister never left his bedside, except to use the restroom, and to change into new dresses the CCU nurses had purchased. They each had a rosary in their hands. They sat side by side with their heads bowed for hours. His father would make frequent brief visits and then leave the room with tear-filled eyes.

"Father's heart is broken," Maria whispered to Stanley. "He said he has killed his only son."

Those prayers were answered at approximately 11:30 on the morning of the third day.

A wide-eyed 13 year old Mexican girl, wearing a sky blue cotton dress, covered with a sunflower design, came running out of unit four screaming, "His foot hurts; he said his foot hurts very much!"

Ciao's brown eyes darted around the room from one piece of medical equipment to the next, wide-eyed as his mother kissed him repeatedly on the forehead. He softly whimpered.

His mother whispered, staring into her son's eyes while she stroked his face with her right hand.

"Mother is telling my brother of a miracle from Mother Mary," Maria said to Stanley, "and from Jesus. He is her miracle son."

Stanley went to the waiting room and found the father.

"He's awake. Ciao is awake. Ciao...Come...COME!" Stanley repeated several times and then reached out his left hand and led this giant of a man to see his little son whose death he had silently been mourning since the accident.

He became a sobbing hulk. An indelible picture formed for all present: Mother on the right side of the bed standing over her son looking into his eyes and speaking softly in Spanish, Father kneeling on the left side of the bed holding his son's hand and praying out loud a prayer of thanks in Spanish, and his sister Maria standing next to her mother with tears flowing and dripping from her chin.

Now Stanley had known some strong muscular men in his life. On occasion during his college years, he would box with heavyweight division boxers, even though he was light-heavyweight. He knew well their strength. He had never felt a clinch like what happened next.

Unexpectedly, Stanley felt rock hard deltoid muscles and powerful forearms wrapping around him from behind and tightening like a Boa Constrictor in a suffocating embrace. He could feel the father's brachial arteries pulsating rapidly in both arms, and his heart pounding. By turning and tilting his head back, Stanley looked into the grateful man's face. Ciao's father's tear-reddened, soft brown eyes were thanking him in the universal language of love.

Two weeks after the surgery, the surgeon, confident that the wounds were healing without signs of serious infection, discharged the miracle child. Ciao had lived when secretly the entire medical staff caring for him had doubted a good outcome and most thought he would die, that is, until the morning he regained consciousness. He had survived severe hemorrhage and shock. Ciao was seen weekly on an outpatient basis in the Emergency Room until the family left the area and returned to Mexico.

They had no insurance and very little money. It really did not matter to anyone involved. Everyone who participated in Ciao's care knew they had just witnessed a very special event. The surgeon, A.W. Blue, refused to submit a bill for his services. Big Bay General Hospital generated a bill for services and then did nothing with it.

The day Ciao was discharged, Maria and her mother approached Stanley.

"Mother would like you to have this." And with that, Ciao's mother pressed a metal medallion of a praying angel into Stanley's right hand.

"I will keep this with me forever," Stanley said as the three of them hugged in unison.

"It feels warm," Stanley told Nancy one morning while holding the medallion after a particularly rough week.

Chapter 6

The Usual Suspects

S tanley loves Poor Joe's Tavern. He practically lived there during his college years, preferring it to the college library as a place to study. The ambiance of the old building that smells of hops and excitement draws him back and comforts him. He finds the history of this two story, white clapboard building fascinating. Now that he was working on the day shift at the hospital, he once again became a regular.

Poor Joe's Tavern is located at the intersection of Union and Basswood in Big Bay. It is in a residential neighborhood. Originally built in 1898 by Irish immigrants, the building served as a whiskey supply depot and trading post. Joe McClain purchased the building in 1929 and converted it to a "dance hall." Joe had lost his right foot in a "boating accident" in 1928. While attempting to jump from the pier to his fishing trawler at 3am after a night of festivities, his foot became lodged between the cement pier and boat. The wave action caused the boat to rock, crushing Joe's foot into mush. The dance hall was "a living."

During Prohibition, Joe reportedly maintained a clandestine still in the basement. He built "apartments" on the second floor above the dance hall, and rented these rooms to "the girls." When questioned about the dubious business practices occurring at the dance hall, Joe replied, "These be hard times and all God's children be entitled."

After the repeal of Prohibition in 1933, the dance hall became a legitimate neighborhood bar and a sign proclaiming the same now hung from the front of the building. The white metal sign with green lettering reads: "Poor Joe's Tavern."

Poor Joe's Tavern is now under the ownership of Timothy Fife. Timothy served with the Special Forces during the Vietnam War, and then as a police detective in St Paul, Minnesota.

Timothy opens for breakfast promptly at 7am each day of the week. He closes officially at 12 midnight. Poor Joe's is his life. His employees are Dora, who comes to work at noon daily to do the cooking, and a large German shepherd dog named Jimmy who lives behind the counter next to the cash register. Jimmy is the alarm system and bar bouncer.

The menu consists of fried perch, chili, Sloppy Joes, deluxe grilled cheese sandwiches, potato chips or potato salad and Dora's famous red hot clam chowder on Fridays. A popcorn maker manufactured in 1928 is located at the west end of the bar. The salty popcorn is free.

The patrons also include residents who rent rooms from Timothy. They live in the rooms upstairs that were formerly rented to the girls.

"The usual suspects," as they love to be called, include Pete, who is a Mekong Delta survivor, as well as Wayne, who is left over from the Korean conflict. Then there is Morris, who lost his right eye in Vietnam, and there is quiet Jonathon.

Jonathon admits he lost his mind in Vietnam, and sits at the table in the southwest corner of Poor Joe's so he can view everyone as they first enter the building while he sips on Black Label beer from 7am to 12 midnight every day. Jonathon keeps a wooden baseball bat leaning against the wall in that corner, behind the window drapes.

Jonathon believes he was born different. From his earliest memories, he felt sorry for those around him. He was born in a small farming village called Buckley. His father, like most of the men in the vicinity, labored as a subsistence farmer, barely providing for his family from year to year. One year after an especially poor, drought-plagued growing season, Jonathon asked his father, "Why don't you do something different?" He received a spanking for being disrespectful. He was seven.

Jonathon's father farmed using a 1947 John Deere B tractor. One summer day while pulling a heavy hay wagon filled to capacity towards the barn, the John Deere sputtered twice and quit running. Jonathan watched as the assembled men mused about the possible causes of this calamity, bemoaning the costs of repairs. Jonathan walked up to the men and announced, "I can fix it," to the guff-haws of the farmers. His father gave a depressed shrug and said, "Have a go at it, but if you break anything, you'll get a whopping." Jonathon rebuilt the John Deere carburetor, and the tractor started with the third turn of the flywheel. He was fifteen.

When he graduated from high school, he announced that he wanted to attend college. His mother, who had completed her formal education at grade eight, told him, "We're not college folks here. "

Jonathon knew that meant the family had no money. He hugged his mother, and told her, "Things will work out." He left home and joined the Army.

After boot camp, Jonathon was assigned to the Army Mechanical and Ordinance Battalion at Fort Lee, Virginia. Two years later he found himself in Saigon, South Vietnam. On June 8th, 1972, his battalion was on the outskirts of Trang Bang watching the Air Force drop napalm on the village. A hot humid tropical wind blew the smell of burning petroleum mixed with burning rubber and burnt flesh from the village into the soldiers' faces. The smoke made the soldiers eyes burn and water. Soon, villagers were running towards them, women carrying burnt children, and naked children running towards them with their clothing burnt away.

The realization that human beings could treat each other in such a horrendous manner caused Jonathon's coping mechanisms to completely implode. Two months later the United States Army discharged Jonathon with a section eight mental disability.

The Roster of the usual suspects at Poor Joe's is completed by Ralph. Ralph showed up one Sunday morning, barefoot, carrying a brown suitcase and a trumpet in a canvas bag. He thinks he was in the Navy because of his tattoos. Every morning at 7am he plays the national anthem while facing the stars and stripes hanging on the east wall of Poor Joe's while Timothy prepares breakfast. Jonathon always stands at attention, along with the guard dog Jimmy, until the playing is completed.

Stanley admires these men.

Tuesday had been a rough day in the Coronary Care Unit. Stanley had worked an extra four hours after a young man in his 40's was admitted following a cardiac arrest. The efforts to save the man eventually proved futile.

That evening he walked from his house to Poor Joe's, trying to clear his mind of the day's chaos. Stanley strolled into Poor Joe's exhausted and a little depressed.

All eyes in Poor Joes' were staring at the 25 inch color television located over the bar next to the Winston clock. As Stanley walked towards the bar, the television showed a Marine in dress uniform bending over and talking to a young blond lady sitting at the grave site. She had a small blond haired child in her arms and her body was shaking with sobs as the Marine handed her the folded flag that had covered her husband's coffin.

"I hate war," Stanley muttered to the assembled vets while Taps was being played at the funeral.

"Well fuck you," replied Pete.

"Yeah….and the pony you rode in on," chimed in Jonathon.

"War is the manifestation of all that is evil," retorted Stanley.

"Sure, like you know anything about it nurse boy," from the southwest corner.

"Manifestation…..manifestation…..manifestation... that's a college word I bet," muttered Ralph.

"I think I'll just whip your ass," slurred an obviously intoxicated Jonathon.

"Sit down Jonathon!" commanded Timothy from behind the bar. "You couldn't whip Stanley on your best day, trust me."

"Unless you bring your bat," Stanley laughed as he turned away from the television.

"I'm sorry fellas. I only know what war has done to my friends and for that I hate it. Not saying we shouldn't defend ourselves from bullies with evil intent," Stanley continued, "I just see the resulting injuries and deep pains.

"And," Stanley said slowly while watching Jonathon, "it breaks my heart that protesters spit on you when you came home."

Except for the popping coming from the popcorn machine, the television, and the thumping of Jimmy's tail hitting against the leg of Timothy's tall wooden bar stool, the room was silent. The men stared at Stanley, dumbfounded.

Jonathon started to stand up from his corner table. "Yup, I think I'll whip your ass; you don't know shit," he said as he reached for his bat.

Jimmy came out from behind the bar with his tail straight back.

Timothy shouted from behind the bar, "Round of drinks on the house....your choice!"

Jonathon slumped back into his chair, squeezing the bat between his knees.

Stanley took a tall glass of Basil Hayden's bourbon and hopped up on the bar, sitting facing the men. Timothy came out from behind the bar and sat at the table with Ralph.

"I want to tell you guys some true stories," Stanley began.

Pete groaned.

"And the drinks are on me until closing time," Stanley continued.

"That's better," someone said.

"I have known hundreds of vets from six different wars," Stanley stated. "I'm going to tell you a little about one man from each war, starting with the Spanish-American War. I personally took care of each of these brave men."

"Story time," blurted Ralph.

"Shut up Ralph, let 'em tell us," retorted Morris, glaring with his one good eye.

"The first vet I ever took care of was named Lawrence. He had fought in Cuba during the Spanish-American War in 1898. He was a patient in a nursing home and I was a first year nursing student."

"Did they make you wear a nursey cap?" laughed Pete.

"Most of the time Lawrence would sit alone by the south windows of the solarium on the 3rd floor. He had dementia and had rambling conversations with persons we couldn't see. Everybody, including the other patients, considered him a nut case."

"He was ninety years old when I took care of him. He was twenty when he fought in Cuba.

"Did you ever see Teddy Roosevelt?" I asked him one day.

"He looked up at me and said, 'Of course I saw Teddy Roosevelt.'

"I soon discovered that the old man loved to play checkers, and was very good at it too. Every afternoon at 2pm Lawrence would have the checker board in place on a card table and 'loaded,' waiting for me to sit down and play. I would usually loose."

"You mean that old man could whip your butt, college boy?" asked Dora.

"He could, Dora.

"It was during these checker matches that he would talk about the war he had fought 68 years ago.

"'Santiago de Cuba is a beautiful place. I would have loved to go back and to live there, but we had a farm and father needed my help after the war,' he told me, with regret in his voice.

"'The Cubans are beautiful and laugh and smile even during the war; so many died. The yellow fever and the infection killed many people. The ladies were beautiful and their men very brave. I talk to them when they stop by and they tell me everything is fine now... so many of my friends from then; they are my good friends....'

"And he would just drift back to Santiago de Cuba for a few minutes and his brown eyes would become very sad."

"Did he go up that hill with Teddy?" asked Pete.

"He told me that he did Pete, and that Roosevelt was like a crazy man, and that he was wounded in that battle, but paid no attention to it."

"How about World War One, my Grandfather was in World War One!" exclaimed Jonathon from his table.

"World War One, Jonathon. Let me tell you about Willard. He was admitted to the heart unit with bad breathing problems. When I asked him how long he had been having lung problems he answered, 'Since 1918.

"'I was in the Great War,' he told me. 'I was in the trenches in France.'

"Willard told me in a very slow voice, 'When it rained, the mud in the trenches would be half-way to our knees. It was a mixture of piss, shit and cigarette butts and empty cans and other stuff. Most of us had infections on our skin and between our toes.

"'It was a relief when we would hear the artillery fire because we knew they had missed our spot. The explosions came before the sound of the guns you know.

"'The worst was the mustard gas. The other explosions would kill some of us right then and there and that was the end of it. The damn mustard gas explosions were a softer thud and the gas would drift to the low spots and down the trenches and the guys would be putting on the masks and crying out that their eyes were burning and their lungs were on fire.

"'Mustard gas....didn't kill me, just left me a lung cripple for all these years; can't even climb a flight of stairs.'

"And then," Stanley continued, "He leaned closer to me and told me, 'We were more scared than you can ever imagine.'

"The look in his eyes told me that he still was."

"Did he make it?" asked Ralph.

"No Ralph, he did not."

And with that Ralph opened the canvas bag always at his side, removed his trumpet, stood up and played Taps.

"Tell us about another Vet, Stanley," Dora asked as she was scrubbing burnt chili from the stove's back burner.

"Ok, let me tell you about a guy named Vernon," Stanley continued.

"Who was Vernon?" asked Morris.

"He resembled Teddy Roosevelt with a military flat top haircut," Stanley began.

"Vernon was not a tall man, probably 5'7", and he weighed about 200 pounds. He was hard as rock without any excess fat and he still carried himself in a military fashion.

"At age 17 he lied to get into the Navy with his older brothers. He told me his battleship had escorted an aircraft carrier to Hawaii after Pearl Harbor. That aircraft carrier later launched the air attack which shot down Yamamoto Isoroku's plane over the Solomon Islands."

"Who?" asked Dora.

"The Mastermind of Japan's attack on Pearl Harbor.

"I got to know Vernon as a patient. He invited me to stop by and chat after he was discharged. Heck, I'm single and had plenty of time so I would. He lived in a garage that had been converted to a rental apartment. We became pretty good friends and I would stop by once a week and check on him. Vernon would always have prepared a meal and we would talk for hours.

"On this particular day there was no food simmering on the stove and the oven was cold. Vernon was sitting at the little round kitchen table with a bottle of Wild Turkey Bourbon Whiskey and a shot glass in front of him. Today was the 'anniversary day,' just as it had been every year for the past 60 years.

"'We were on a search and destroy mission off the coast of Okinawa and the Jap Zeros came at us full speed just above the water,' he told me.

"'Most of the planes got right through our machine gun fire and two of them hit the starboard side and everything blew up.'

"Then Vernon lifted a shot glass filled with Wild Turkey and slowly savored a mouthful before swallowing. I watched as he closed his eyes and let the Kentucky spirits flow through his aging body.

"'It blew part of the bow right off,' Vernon said.

"He was a 17 year old sailor watching the terrible day happening again.

"'I watched my buddy Harry crawl using his arms across the deck towards me. His legs were mutilated and there was a trail of blood. His face looked at me with a terrified look. Then another plane hit us and Harry was gone in a ball of fire. All those boys screaming from down below deck.... it was awful. They were trapped and burning.' He shivered and slowly sighed and then a lone tear trickled down his weathered left cheek," Stanley continued.

"'They were fine friends of mine,' Vernon said.

"Then Vernon pushed the old cork back into the bottle of Wild Turkey. He carefully placed it back in the cupboard to wait for next year.

"'How about I just go get us some Kentucky Fried Chicken tonight Vern?' I asked him.

"'I would like that, and some mashed potatoes with that gravy of theirs and some biscuits...long as you don't tell Doc,' he said.

"'I promise,' I told him.

"It was on a Saturday afternoon when I received a phone call from his daughter. She told me that her father had died yesterday and that she had found him sitting in his chair.

"'Dad had a big manila envelope on his kitchen table with your name and telephone number on it,' she said."

"What was in it.....tell us," slurred Jonathon.

"The first thing I found when I reached into that old military envelope was a black and white Kodak picture of a proud young sailor standing next to a heavy machine gun mounted on the bow of a United States Navy Destroyer.

"Then I pulled out several military medals. One of the medals was a Purple Heart.

"The very last thing I found in the envelope was a two dollar bill. I put that two dollar bill into the secret compartment of my wallet."

And with that, Stanley removed his wallet from his back pocket, opened it and removed a two dollar bill with a red government seal for all to examine.

"Damn, that poor guy lived through some terror," commented Dora.

"Sure did," agreed Pete.

"We all have," Timothy quietly said from his chair. "We all have."

"How about from my war?" clambered Wayne. "Did you ever take care of any guys from my war?"

"I have Wayne."

"You guys would have really liked Ellsworth. He was a Korean War vet, like you Wayne. He was a quiet man who spoke only when spoken to. He came to the hospital because of heart failure.

"I was attempting to complete his medical history which was arduous since Ellsworth answered most questions with a yes or a no whenever possible.

"Then I asked him about the tattoo on his right forearm and he launched back to August 1950.

"'I was in the infantry and we were dug in at the 38th parallel and then all hell broke loose on us. The Koreans and Chinese just kept coming in waves and we keep pulling back until we ended up in Pusan and the Pacific was at our back.

"'They had Russian weapons.

"'We finally drove them back across the 38th. It was a bloody cold mess and there were times when I even felt sorry for those fellas on the other side who didn't want to be there either. Some of us boys talked about how much more fun it would be if we could drink a beer with them instead of shooting at each other, but then the shooting would start again and some of us would be hit.

"'The worst day was when we were being shelled and one exploded quite close, knocking me on my back. When I gathered my wits about me and tried to sit up, I felt an arm resting on my chest. I spit the mud out of my mouth and rolled over. The wrist watch on the arm said it was 3:17. It was my buddy Jake's watch that his wife had sent him last Christmas! *Oh no... I thought... oh no, not Jake, he just got married the week before de-*

ployment.

"'Jake's eyes were open and filled with mud. His mouth was filled with mud. His left arm had been blown right off. He was dead. I lay beside him for a long time and cried as I wiped the mud and blood off his face. I poured water from my canteen and washed the mud out of Jakes eyes and then I took my fingers and closed them.'

"Then Ellsworth looked at me and said, 'Well sir, the good news is that that was the worst day of my life. The bad news is that I remember it every single day.'"

Poor Joe's was silent except for the late night newscast on the TV over the bar. Then Wayne stood up and walked over to Stanley sitting on the bar.

"I'm sorry we gave you shit when you came in man, truly sorry. What that Ellsworth said to you was right."

"Can I play Taps for Ellsworth and Vern now?" asked Ralph.

"Yes," was the answer in unison.

Ralph stood up and played Taps again just as Wendell walked through the front door.

"Who died?" Wendell asked.

"Lots of guys. Stanley is telling us about Vets he has taken care of Wendell; sit down and listen," Jonathon commanded.

"Actually you know this guy, Wendell. Remember Doug?"

"Oh yeah!"

"Let me tell you guys about Doug. He served in Vietnam, like you, Timothy.

"I had arrived at the hospital early, 5am, to work on the staffing schedule and finish a budget report before the day got busy.

"Then my pager went off: 'Code Gray. Step Down Unit.' Then second page: 'Call Step Down Stat.'"

"What's a Code Gray?" asked Dora

"Code Gray is code for a combative patient.

"I ran to this Code Gray. I don't even run to Code Blues, but I ran to this. The night shift was staffed with young nurses and I was pretty certain I knew who was causing the problem.

"Doug had been a Special Forces Marine. By his own account he had been a participant in many intense battles during the early years of the Vietnam War, even before it became widely known in the U.S., at times against an enemy that was 'less than obvious.' He admitted that women and children had been casualties; 'Could never know when they had a bomb strapped on them.' Those occasions gave Doug nightmares which crippled him.

"And to add to the tragic waste, Doug had a brilliant mind--a photographic memory--and could quote page number and paragraph of any book he had ever read.

"With his return to civilian life, Doug found himself completely unable to focus and settle on a career. 'I guess I've been a Jack of all Trades,' he told me. 'Let's see...I've been a handyman, a carpenter and roofer, a short order cook and auto mechanic and I had a lawn care business in Florida for a couple of years.'

"This time Doug had been admitted for treatment of alcoholic cardiomyopathy; a severe weakening of the heart muscle caused by excessive drinking. 'I've had therapy and rehab and pills and the only thing that really works for me is alcohol and I really like the way it makes me feel,' he said.

"'Alcohol helps me, I like it,' he had told me when he was admitted."

"I like it too!" shouted Jonathon from his corner table.

"We know Jonathon," replied Timothy with a little smile on his face.

"I ran up the stairs and down the hall and around the corner to the Step-Down Unit. And there was Doug, standing at the west end of the hallway, wearing a blue hospital gown; it was not tied in the back. He had a wet floor mop in both hands, waving it in a circular fashion over his head as he advanced towards four frightened young nurses and two semi-brave orderlies.

"When Doug spotted me, he stopped swinging the mop and began counting. 'One... two... three... four... five... six...,' and then pointing at me, 'seven. You guys are going to need more help,' he said as he began to swing the mop again.

"I said to him, 'What the hell are you doing Doug? Look at this mess and you have all these ladies upset and by the way the janitor needs his mop back so give it here. What's wrong anyway?'

"'Damn it! Damn, damn, sonofabitch. They won't let me call my mom. Shit anyway.'

"'You got her number?' I asked him. 'I'll call her myself,' he said. I put my right arm around him and we walked past the orderlies and back to the nurses' station. I handed him the phone and dialed the number for him.

"'Sorry,' he said. I just needed to talk to my mom and nobody would listen.'

"He tried to call her several times without an answer. 'Well I guess they weren't lying; Blondie said she tried to call, but I don't trust them. I don't trust any of them.'

"I spent another two hours in Doug's room, talking to him instead of getting the schedules completed. Doug's poor mind jumped from thought to thought like a stone being skipped on still water. I felt so sorry for him.

"He told me, 'I was covered with Agent Orange...2-4-5-T just so you know; lots of times, and who the hell knew what we were smoking, but it helped some.'

"That afternoon he was transferred to a Veterans' hospital."

Stanley took another long sip of Basil Hayden's.

"I'll bet you've known lots of Dougs," Jonathon commented. "I'm sorry for what I said to you about your pony."

Then Stanley jumped down off the bar. Jimmy came over with his tail wagging and Stanley poured some of Ralph's beer on the floor for him to lap up.

"Fellas, I have been over-served and I must go home now. I meant no disrespect and I'm sorry if I hurt any feelings here tonight.

"Good night my friends."

As Stanley headed for the door; Wendell, Pete, Wayne, Morris,

Jonathon, Ralph and Timothy lined up and shook his hand. Dora gave him a big hug.

"You guys have paid a price for our freedom that most of us cannot fathom," Stanley said as he saluted his friends.

Jimmy the guard dog walked with Stanley the seven blocks to Stanley's house on Grant Street and then trotted back to Poor Joe's Tavern to help Timothy close up for the night.

Chapter 7

Broken Bodies

T hings had been quiet at Big Bay General ever since Chief had interrupted the night orderly and a nurse's aide in the linen closet. Chief had guided the orderly, whose name was Pete, to the nurses' station by his left earlobe while the flustered nurse's aide, named Ruth, "put herself back together." Ruth then frantically gathered her personal belongings from the nurses' locker room and left the hospital.

Weeks later Wendell found Ruth waiting tables at Mark's Diner on Basswood Street. "She seemed happy working at the diner, and told me she's dating Pete."

Romance is not uncommon in the hospital environment. Some of the romance is honorable. Some of the escapades would not be something you would mention to your mother.

The hospital setting is almost a perfect storm for interludes and occasions of afternoon delight. There are men and there are women. Then add the fact that these men and women spend more time with each other than they do with their spouses. It is a recipe for all sorts of mischief and adolescent sexual adventures regardless of the participants' given ages. In many ways these adventures provide an escape from the reality of the stressful lives being lived both at the hospital and at home.

It had been almost a year since Dr. A.W. Blue emptied his bank accounts and took the money as well as his office nurse, Rita, and traveled to Key West, Florida. He left his wife, Carole, the house and all accounts receivables. This financial settlement was not satisfactory to Carole Blue or her lawyers. When a private detective hired by Mrs. Blue showed up in Key West asking questions about A.W., the Dr. and Rita hired a charter boat to transport them to an unnamed Caribbean island.

When questioned in court, the charter captain, whose name was Quinn O'Malley, did not recall ever having met the Doctor. There was no finical record in the legers of such a trip having ever taken place.

It is the stuff that legends are made of and not a rare occurrence either, sad as that may be.

The Big Bay rumor lines once again hummed. A new Registered Nurse had been hired, which is not that newsworthy. However, this nurse had been hired by the Hospital Administrator as a favor to an old friend, neglecting the Director of Nurses, who reportedly became "really, really pissed." She threatened to resign.

The Board of Directors stepped into their little war, giving the Director of Nurses a significant increase in her salary and extracting an apology from the Administrator.

Then the much anticipated Monday arrived and the new nurse walked into the CCU accompanied by the Director of Nursing.

"I want you all to meet our new CCU nurse. Her name is Danielle. Welcome Danielle. I'm sure you will love it here at Big Bay as much as we love having you here." And with that, the Director was gone, leaving the most beautiful lady Stanley had ever seen, standing in the middle of the CCU.

Their eyes met and locked and Danielle smiled a quick smile with her hazel eyes. It seemed at that moment they had known each other for a very long time and Stanley's heart was pounding.

Danielle had moved to Big Bay from New Orleans, where her father was a hospital administrator. She had a boyfriend who lived in Alaska.

She became an instant hit with the CCU staff. As smart as she was beautiful, Danielle did not seem to realize that she was either.

As the days and weeks and months passed, Danielle and Stanley said very little to each other, except for the routine medical and nursing conversations. The occasional brief looks they caught themselves sharing together made each feel uncomfortable.

The ongoing nursing shortage made it difficult to recruit nurses from other hospitals. In an attempt to have a more versatile nursing staff, the Director of Nursing decided to create a new department titled Critical Care, and to educate a pool of Critical Care Nurses able to work in CCU/ICU, the Recovery Room, and the Emergency Room.

She called Stanley to her office.

"Stan I would like you to be the Head Nurse for this new Critical Care Nursing pool I'm working on."

"I would like that very much, Ramona."

"Good. I thought you would and you can teach better than anyone else I know."

"Thank you. I enjoy teaching. It's a great way for me to learn too."

"Set up a preceptor program. It'll take some of the pressure off you, and the staff will be more inclined to take ownership."

"Good idea."

"And," Ramona continued, "I want you to be the preceptor for Danielle. I was wrong about that young lady. I had my nose bent out of shape, but you know all about that. She's going far in our profession. You can teach her a lot."

Stanley sucked in a quick involuntary breath, stunned by the request. "Thank You," was his only response.

After three weeks of class preparation, the Director of Nursing launched the new staffing system. Stanley and Danielle began their rotation together in the Emergency Room on the midnight shift.

The first patient walked through the ER door shortly after midnight. He was a "Harley rider" who had the misfortune of trying to drink a Stroh's beer, eat a pizza and turn at an intersection just west of Big Bay General, all at the same time.

"I dumped the hog," was his introduction to the problem, as he walked through the Emergency Room entrance. It was obvious that he had slid through the gravel at a considerable speed. Long shreds of skin dangled from his left arm. The gravel embedded in his forehead, arms and chest gave him a Halloween appearance.

From his right hand drooped a dirt-infested pepperoni pizza which he ate as he spoke, spitting out the occasional pebble.

"Just need a few Band-Aids," was the rider's request.

Danielle left the nurses' station and took him to ER Room Two. Together Stanley and Danielle cut the remains of his muscle shirt away. For the next hour they carefully picked gravel from the biker's wounds. Danielle washed the abrasions with Hydrogen Peroxide and an iodine solution. The ER Doctor came in, ordering an antibiotic and tetanus shot then left just as the police who had found a Harley motorcycle in the middle of the intersection arrived looking for the rider.

"Honey if you give me your phone number I'll give you a call when I'm healed up and thank you properly," was the biker's parting comment to Danielle, as two policemen escorted him to the back seat of the patrol car.

"Bye now," is all she said.

And that was just the beginning of their first shift in the Emergency Room together.

Maybe from all those years of boxing and facing improbable situations or maybe his genetic disposition, the worse a situation, the calmer Stanley became. Utter chaos found him absolutely focused on the task before him. The time was 6:30 in the morning and Stanley was about to become very calm.

The Sheriff's Department called on the ER hotline saying there had been a multiple car accident on the highway five miles west of town and there were at least six people badly injured.

Danielle took the call on the red phone. She turned to Stanley at the end of the conversation. "I'm glad you're on tonight," is all she said as she picked up the intercom phone to call ICU and the ER Doctor's sleeping room.

There had been a five vehicle accident during the morning rush hour. A semi-truck hit a compact car head-on. Two pickups and a Corvette also crashed into the wreckage. The Corvette, driven by a prominent Big Bay business owner, ended up lodged under the semi- trailer and burst into flames.

Four ambulances pulled into the ER within ten minutes of each other. The first three came up the drive to Big Bay General with their lights and sirens on. The fourth drove up slowly; it was transporting the Corvette driver.

The two pickup drivers had non-life threatening injuries. The semi-truck driver had first and second degree burns on both hands and forearms.

Three young ladies had been in the compact car. They all worked in the hospital cafeteria.

Their bodies were broken and twisted beyond belief. The staff in the ER worked feverously as their hearts were breaking. Even the steely natured ER physician was teary-eyed as he worked. All three ladies died before they could be taken to the operating rooms.

Danielle and Stanley pushed the gurney with the last young cafeteria worker to the morgue. They placed her next to her two co-workers and the Corvette driver. Side by side they stood in that cold room together while trying to comprehend the tragedy of this awful morning.

After a few minutes they returned to the ER and worked for another hour, helping the day shift clean up the considerable mess.

"You were magnificent," Danielle whispered as she left to go home.

"We both were," Stanley replied. He meant it. He had never seen such composure by a young nurse.

Thankfully, the next month in the ER remained quiet with the usual cases of sprains, cuts, diaper rash and influenza. Danielle and Stanley grew closer with each passing shift and they both knew it without saying a single word on the subject.

One morning their hands clasped together, transferring a patient from an ambulance stretcher to the ER table. They looked into each other's eyes the moment their hands touched. Instantly Danielle's checks flushed and she felt warm over her entire body. Stanley's skin tingled everywhere, and his heart palpated. Neither of them wanted to let go.

Together they rode this teeter-totter, trying to maintain proper behavior and decorum despite the fury raging in their souls. Even being in the same room together was a distraction to both of them and they secretly wondered if anyone else could tell.

Stanley was in his office, located down the hall from the CCU, working on the staffing schedule when Danielle walked in.

"Do you have a minute?" she asked.

"Sure."

"I need two weeks off, next month if possible please."

"I think we can free you up next month."

"I need to fly to Alaska."

Chapter 8

Night Security

T hose who believe that the full moon has no effect on human beings are misinformed. It is like the ancient ones who did not understand that ultraviolet radiation from the sun causes sunburn. Sometimes all we can do with our limited understanding is observe the effects that occur.

The full moon was bright overhead and the moon glow shining through apple trees cast strange shadows on the hospital lawn. The ER was just nuts. Alcoholics and those who were near contenders populated the waiting room with a wide variety of problems, all of which would be fixed with "pain pills."

Domestic disturbances blossomed. A man made brave and adventurous by ample amounts of adult beverages, staggered into the ER after being hit on the head with a cast iron frying pan by his wife when he brought a lady friend home from Poor Joe's, suggesting they all have a party.

The Big Bay police were busy. A knife fight had erupted at Jen's

Place, a downtown night spot popular with the college kids. A young man working on his PhD had commented to a group of Harley riders from New York City, "You scholars have an Intelligence Quotient that's room temperature."

The bikers took exception to this comment. All common sense had long been extinguished by alcohol. A fight quickly ensued. The bikers used Bowie knives and the college kids used chairs.

The knives won.

The bikers quickly left town after the successful defense of their honor. Someone noticed the back of the bikers' leather jackets proclaiming them as "HELL'S SPAWN."

Nine college students came to the ER with an assortment of lacerations. Six cut up young men and three young ladies, all bleeding and all of them quite drunk.

Stanley called the CCU and two nurses were sent to help.

It was Nancy's turn for the ER preceptor rotation, as part of the Critical Care Pool. Stanley liked Nancy. He admired her kind and forgiving spirit, and her gentleness. And when they were together, Stanley felt protective of Nancy since the terrible beating she received from the alcoholic patient that opening night of the first Coronary Care Unit. She was a very good nurse, but somewhat of a mystery as a person. She lived in a house which she purchased on a hill overlooking the bay. She owned two Cocker Spaniels, named Salem and Spirit, and a German Shepard she called "Manley." Nancy also owned a parakeet she named "Richard," after the only man she had ever loved.

Stanley and Nancy made a great team. They worked together in synchrony, treating the injuries in order of seriousness. Just as it seemed that they were about caught up, a pregnant lady came running through the ER door.

She ran past the ER nurses' station and towards the elevators, leaving a trail of amniotic fluid on the floor as she traveled. Pete, the night orderly, was right behind her. Ruth was about to have a baby!

The elevator doors opened. Pete pushed the number four button for the Maternity Ward just as Nancy and Stanley barged through the closing elevator doors. Ruth sank to the floor and spread her legs wide apart as she proclaimed, "here it comes." First, a little black haired head appeared and with the next contraction an entire baby filled Nancy's hands. The umbilical cord was wrapped around the baby's neck and under the left arm. Stanley quickly and gently ran his forefinger under the baby's arm pit and around the neck to remove the cord.

"Well, congratulations you guys," Nancy exclaimed as the doors opened to the Maternity Ward. She reached for a towel, which one of the Maturity nurses held out, and wrapped the beautiful little girl with it. She placed the baby on Ruth's chest as they were both loaded onto a stretcher.

Wendell was mopping up the ER floor as Stanley and Nancy returned to the ER. "I really do hate full moon nights," Stanley commented to no one in particular. The shift would be over soon.

Several of the day shift nurses had arrived when Timothy came charging through the ER doors carrying Jimmy. Jimmy's ears pointed up when he spotted Stanley, and his tail started to wag. Blood dripped from a wound in his left hind leg, leaving a trail of little red splatters on the floor.

"Jimmy's been shot!" Timothy exclaimed to Stanley as he walked into ER Room Three and laid the German Shepard on the stretcher. "You guys save him." It was not a request.

"Who shot him?" Stanley asked.

"Some crazy bastard! Jonathon and Wayne have him out in the car.....back seat."

"Is he hurt Timothy?" Stanley asked.

"Jimmy and Jonathon beat him up pretty good."

Stanley and one of the CCU nurses took a stretcher to the ER entrance and found the man being held in a strangle hold by Jonathon. The man was semiconscious. With a little persuasion, Stanley convinced Jonathon to release the patient. Examination in ER Room One found his injuries to be multiple and significant.

The man had numerous puncture and bite wounds on both arms, on the right side of his neck, his left buttock and left calf muscle. He also had a large contusion over his left eye and that eye was swollen shut.

No one knew the man. Evidently a vagrant who had wandered into town during the night, he had decided to rob Poor Joe's in the early morning hours.

Gaining entry had not been difficult. Timothy never locked Poor Joe's for two reasons: he did not want any of the nearly one hundred year old glass broken with forced entry, and Jimmy was inside.

Jimmy never made a sound as the vagrant entered through the front door and walked behind the bar to the cash register. Then in a flash, the man was knocked to the floor by a ninety pound German Shepard. A ferocious fight ensued on the floor behind the bar, which awakened Jonathon who had passed out at his designated table.

The vagrant struggled to his feet while pulling a small handgun from his blue jean jacket pocket. He shot Jimmy, striking him in the left front leg. At that same instant, the intruder became aware of a presence behind him. As the man turned to his left with his gun raised, Jonathon hit him in the forehead with a baseball bat.

The fact that the intruder went unconscious probably saved his life. The racket and gunshot had summoned all the residents from upstairs. Timothy stroked Jimmy's head as he tried to assess the extent of the injuries. Jimmy cried out when Timothy touched the wounded leg, then tried to lick the wound. Seeing his best friend crying out in pain and bleeding, it took every bit of his self-control for Timothy not to stand up and stomp on the shooter's head. Wayne, Morris, Pete and Ralph stood over the unconscious man, trying to decide the next course of action. Jonathon stood with his baseball bat at the ready.

"Well damn it all anyway! Should we just bury him?" asked Ralph.

"Not till he's dead," replied Wayne. "Well wait. He broke into our place; let's just call the police."

The police were always a last option for them.

"We have to go to the hospital. Jimmy's been shot; let's take my car and go to the ER and see Stanley. He'll know what to do," Timothy said.

Wayne drove the 1956 Buick. The automobile was seldom used. Timothy rarely traveled and saw no reason to replace the broken driver's side headlight and worn-out brakes. It had not had a muffler for many years. A car of this vintage and shape had been part of his cover during his detective career. Timothy sat up front, cradling Jimmy in his arms. The boys lugged the unconscious intruder to the back seat where Wayne and Jonathon guarded their prisoner. Jonathon held him in a chokehold learned long ago in the Army, just in case.

The ER Doctor probed Jimmy's wound and decided it was a "through and through ....nothing vital hit." Stanley shaved the hair away from the entrance and exit wounds, applied antibiotic ointment, and then wrapped the leg with gauze to keep him from licking it. Nancy quickly gave him an IM antibiotic. Then the boys carried Jimmy to the Buick for the trip back to Poor Joe's.

No paperwork was generated for the veterinary services provided.

The vagrant did not fare as well as Jimmy. The "justice" rendered by Jimmy and the fellows resulted in a three week ICU stint, prior to being escorted to the county jail where he awaited trial.

"Hey thanks for your help Stanley," Timothy said as they shook hands. "Who's the new girl and where's Danielle?"

"That's Nancy. She's been here for several years....just starting in the ER.

"Danielle is on vacation in Alaska."

Chapter 9

Blanche Marie's Return Trip

B ig Bay General now had three Cardiologists. The newest member of the team, Jack Kennedy McCaferty was a dark curly haired Irish boy to the very soul. He was an easy fit for the city of Big Bay which is predominately populated by folks of Irish descent.

And his very first cardiac patient at Big Bay General was on a stretcher in the Emergency Room.

"Stanley would you meet me in the ER; we have a lady with Mobitz 2 heart block," said Dr. McCaferty on the phone.

"Be right down Doctor."

"Please call me Jack."

"On my way Jack."

Blanche Marie Kozlowski was 94 years old. She had been a widow for seven years, and lived with her son, Randy, at his house located just down the hill from Nancy. Her son had called Nancy at home, stating, "Mom keeps passing out and waking up and passing out again.

"She's lying on the kitchen floor right now," he added. "She says she's not hurt."

"Keep her flat right there on the floor. Don't let her get up. I'll call an ambulance. I'll be right there Randy," Nancy instructed.

In the ER, the EKG monitor showed sudden episodes of complete heart block and a very slow ventricular escape rhythm. During these intermittent episodes of heart block, Blanche Marie's blood pressure could not be found and she would lose consciousness.

Dr. McCaferty was explaining the critical nature of the situation to Blanche Marie and her son as Stanley entered ER Room Four.

"She needs to be set up for a temporary pacemaker and scheduled for a permanent this afternoon," Dr. McCaferty said to Stanley. "I checked; there is a patient in the Cath Lab right now."

"I'll call the CCU and have them set up for a temporary and have the Cath Lab hold the next scheduled patient," Stanley replied.

Blanche Marie was transported by stretcher to the CCU.

Dr. McCaferty and Stanley entered CCU Room Three with the anticipation of placing a temporary cardiac pacemaker. They found the 94 year old patient with the head of her bed in the sitting position. She had a bath blanket wrapped about her shoulders and was wearing reading glasses halfway down her nose.

She had not signed the permit for the pacemaker.

"Well, are you here for the interview?" she asked Dr. McCaferty.

"I'm sorry, do you have further questions?" he replied

"My only question is… are you qualified?" she said with her head tilted back, viewing the doctor through the reading glasses.

Stanley moved to the head of the bed and leaned over close to Blanche.

"Dr. McCaferty has done several hundred pacemakers before ever coming to our hospital. He is one of the most qualified Cardiologists in the country."

"Well good for him. I am not interested," she retorted.

"Blanche you will die if we do not put this pacemaker in you,"

Stanley explained.

Again, the look through the reading glasses.

"I plan on dying, don't you?

"I am 94 years old," she continued. "Give me a break; my parts are dying by bits and pieces. You guys want to put that machine in me so I can watch?"

Dr. McCaferty tried to break the looming stalemate by changing the subject.

"Our nurse Nancy tells me you live down on the bay next to the pier where the ferry docks.

"Has the ferry started running to the Grand Mission yet?" he continued.

"It has," she answered.

Then an awkward pause.

"You interested in ferries are you?" she asked, with a subtle grin on her face.

"Yes I am. I like ferries."

"Why doesn't that surprise me?" And there was now a twinkle in her eyes.

Blanche Marie's heart stopped four hours later at 3:22 that afternoon. Her body was prepared and room tidied up. The nurse's aide pulled the curtains, closing the opening to the room.

Her son Randy had left for a brief trip home to obtain his mother's favorite pillow and personal items. The afternoon charge nurse, Crystal, phoned him. "Your mom is not doing well. Her heart is blocking again and she may not survive this time."

Randy walked in and was met by Dr. McCaferty. "I'm very sorry for your loss. I could tell your mother was a very special lady."

"I'm sorry that your mom died," Crystal told Randy. "You can go in and spend as much time with her as you need."

About ten minutes passed. Then suddenly the curtains were whipped back and the son exclaimed, "Mom wants some prune juice!"

Blanche Marie was sitting straight up in the bed.

DEAD SILENCE.

The only sound in the CCU was that of the ventilator in Room One, making its to and fro breathing sounds.

"Holy shit," escaped from a nurse's aide's lips. Her name was Shannon and she had just completed the post mortem care on Blanche Marie. She had finished by attaching identification tags to the dead lady's right great toe and around her left wrist. "Holy shit...oh my goodness!"

Crystal scampered to the unit kitchen and grabbed a small can of prune juice. She handed it to the son.

The other nurses on duty in the CCU, Sandi and Lisa, walked out of rooms One and Four, staring at Room Three in disbelief. Sandi walked over to the bank of cardiac monitors and turned bed three on. "Let's hook her back up," she exclaimed.

Dr. McCaferty and Stanley stood up from the table in the break room where they were drinking hot tea and discussing the frustrations of Blanche Marie's death.

With her son's help, Blanche Marie drank the entire 3 ounce can of prune juice.

"That tasted real good." And with that, she lay back in bed and closed her eyes for the final time. When Crystal checked for a pulse there was none. The cardiac monitor was quickly reattached and found no cardiac activity.

Water trickled into the sink located below the mirror on the north wall of Blanche Marie's room. It was a white porcelain sink with independent controls for hot or cold on either side of the faucet. Crystal turned the hot water off.

A few minutes later the faucet was again running hot water. Sandi turned it off.

As Sandi had left the room, the hot water faucet turned to the on position again.

Sandi, Lisa, Dr. McCaferty, Stanley, Shannon and Blanche Marie's son stood at the entrance to the room. Crystal turned the hot water off again and took a few steps back.

As they watched, the hot water faucet moved to the on position.

"What!" Crystal exclaimed to no one in particular.

"Crystal, open the window," said Dr. McCaferty, pointing to the west. All six people in that room stared at the faucet as Crystal opened the window.

The faucet remained off after the window in Room Three was opened.

Randy grasped Crystal's left hand and squeezed it very hard as he said, "Mom is with Dad now. They loved each other and Jesus very much."

Crystal turned and wrapped both arms around Randy.

"Yes she is."

Chapter 10

Hugged by an Angel

T he warm August wind smelled clean with a hint of fish as it blew inland from the bay. Stanley met Wendell in the Big Bay General parking lot. Wendell had just finished the night shift and Stanley had arrived for the day shift.

"Hey Stanley, you remember Doug, the Nam Vet who chased you guys with a mop up on Step-Down?" asked Wendell.

"Will never forget that morning."

"Doug called me last night," Wendell said. "He told me he's living in a tent."

"Where?"

"In the swamp on the north side of the river just below the dam," Wendell replied. "Told me he's living on rabbits and trout and Spam. He said he's doing some handyman work like painting and fixing stuff.... will mow a lawn too, if a mower is available."

"I've wondered what happened to Doug. I never heard a thing after we shipped him to the V.A. hospital down state. I felt so bad for him. Geez, that was five years ago."

"Well, we're going to eat supper together at Poor Joe's tomorrow night," Wendell continued. "I'll let you know how he's doing."

Doug and Wendell met on Friday night at 9pm. They both liked clam chowder and were particularly fond of Dora's spicy version; it had Red Hot in the recipe, which required ample amounts of cold draft Schlitz beer as an antidote.

"How the hell you doing out in that tent?" questioned Wendell as they slid into the middle booth on the north wall of Poor Joe's.

"It's a regular 5 star," Doug answered. "I got a mattress and running water and fresh catch on the line anytime I want it."

"You know Doug, in three months it'll be knee deep in snow along the river."

"Yup, been thinking about that. Maybe I should talk to Timothy and see about renting a room upstairs. Most the fellows living here were in Nam just like me; be a good fit I think."

"I was in that hell hole you know," Wendell said.

"I didn't know that Wendell. When did you serve?"

"It was at the end. I was in the U.S. Embassy in Saigon during the evacuation," Wendell answered.

"I caught an MVA grenade that came over the wall like it was a baseball. I threw it back, but it blew just after I let it go," Wendell said as he lifted the remains of his right hand, which consisted of his thumb and forefinger.

"Lucky it didn't blow your head off."

"Still have some of it in my right shoulder and right hip; doesn't bother me much. The hand thing fucked me up pretty good. I had an auto repair business when I was drafted. Came home and damn, couldn't do the wrench work like I should, so ended up as a maintenance man at Big Bay. I sure have missed the garage though."

"Well shit Wendell, I'm real sorry to hear your story. I say let's have some Wild Turkey and talk about stuff."

The two Vietnam Vets talked together like they were in the confessional, revealing pains never before shared with another human while they drank Rum & Cokes, alternating with Wild Turkey.

"I was sent into the mother of all battles on November 8, 1965," Doug said, while staring into Wendell's eyes without blinking. "The 173rd Airborne and some guys from Australia had been ambushed by the VC. Our guys were being slaughtered... I mean...damn; they were taking close fire from all the surrounding hills. The VC even had American made shotguns... it was target practice and our guys were outnumbered. When my platoon reached the valley I could see the angels moving back and forth through the smoke and dust, greeting my brothers' souls. Then one of those angels floated right into my gun turret and wrapped her arms around me. She sang to me in a sweet voice a song I had never heard as she hugged me from behind. Wendell..... I felt invincible. I ordered my corporal to drive the Green Dragon right into the VC positions as I fired the Fifty. The incoming rattled against our armor plates; it sounded like hail from hell. We'd turn around and charge their positions again, over and over; we slid and skidded on VC bodies as we turned ... and then the Air Force swooped in and hellfire rained down and it was over."

"Holy shit! I heard about that ...Operation Hump wasn't it? You're the first guy I've met from that battle."

"Not many of us to meet Wendell....not many. My driver died four days later from a wound he got that day. He's my hero.....he kept on driving with a fist sized hole in his gut. I didn't get a scratch."

"Last call men," Timothy declared from behind the bar.

Pete, Jonathon, Wayne, Morris and Ralph shuffled up the stairs to their rooms. Dora had finished cleaning her kitchen and said, "Goodnight all."

Timothy pulled a chair over and sat down at the end of their booth.

"I have a favor to ask of you Doug," Timothy said as he poured a round of Wild Turkey. "I need a man with your special skill set."

"You need a bartender?" asked Doug. "I'm a good judge of liquor," he bragged, with a big grin on his face.

"That you are, but no. I need a bouncer. Jimmy is twelve years old. His limp from being shot is getting worse. I leave the television on all night as an additional deterrent, but I'm afraid Jimmy would be hurt in another fight."

"Well, thank you Timothy. This means a lot being asked by you. Why me; you know lots of fellows who are younger and bigger than me?"

Timothy finished a second shot of Wild Turkey, took a deep breath. "Doug, you have absolutely no fear in you."

The three men sat at the booth in silence. An infomercial for a life extending elixir was playing on the TV over the bar. Jimmy's tail thumped on the hardwood floor.

"You would have the first room at the top of the stairs," Timothy continued. "Make it easier to hear things at night for you."

Wendell reached across the booth and patted Doug's arm and said, "See, we're being looked out for, even when we don't know it brother."

"Yes….yes I will Timothy. I will accept your offer and I thank you. It will be an honor working with Jimmy."

Timothy called a cab for his friends.

As he was walking up the steps to his home, Wendell thought out loud, "I need to retire."

Chapter 11
Major Decisions

W endell strolled around with a grin on his face and was more animated than usual while making his 2am grocery rounds.

Chief and Cap were sitting in the now smoke-free nurses' station. "I'm going to retire," Wendell announced. "I think I might even sell the house and move to Poor Joe's.....rent a room upstairs with the rest of the guys."

Chief stared at Wendell as if he was a little green space alien.

"You should retire too," Wendell continued, pointing the lone finger in his right hand at Chief. "You're as old as dirt."

"I hope you are about done," retorted Chief. Cap stood up and walked towards the medication room in an effort to escape what appeared to be a looming battle.

"Well Wendell, you make a lot of sense for a man who tried walking on water to go ice fishing."

Chief continued as if talking to the universe, "I've been thinking about it since the day they banned smoking. I enjoy smoking; don't really give a damn if it kills me. I feel like a dinosaur surrounded by transistor babies with all sorts of high degrees in things I can't even pronounce."

Then Chief took a deep breath as she turned to face Wendell. "And I'm tired."

"We sure could have one hell of a retirement party," exclaimed Wendell. He felt relieved that his head remained attached to his neck.

"Yup, Chief, we could have one hell of a party."

* * *

Wendell stood outside the ER entrance, waiting in a gentle morning rain for Stanley.

"Good Morning Wendell, how did it go with Doug Saturday night?"

"I'm retiring."

Stanley and Wendell stood in the warm rain and stared at each other.

"Timothy gave Doug a job at Poor Joe's. He's going to help Jimmy and be a bouncer."

"Oh great…this is going to be special," Stanley replied.

"Yup," Wendell continued, "and Timothy gave Doug the room at the top of the stairs so he could keep track of things. You know, might just be I'll sell the house and get a room there too."

"Yes indeed, this is going to be very special," Stanley said, shaking his head

"Chief is retiring too," Wendell said, saving the best for last. "She's had enough; she told Cap and me that tonight; she's gonna retire too."

"Wow!" exclaimed Stanley. "I see the mother of all retirement parties in our future!"

"Yup…..at Poor Joe's," suggested Wendell.

"Let me work on it." And with that they shook hands and Stanley walked to his office.

* * *

It was 10:17am when Stanley heard the page over the P.A. system, "Outside call…..long distance."

Stanley picked up his desk phone and called the hospital operator named Barb.

"Hi Barb, you have an outside call for me?"

"Sure do, it's Danielle. She's in Seattle between flights and wants to talk to you."

"Great Barb, you going to listen in?" Stanley said in jest.

"Oh come on, I don't do that."

"No really, we want to talk about you."

"Ok silly, here she is."

"Hi Stanley," Danielle said softly.

"Hi Danielle, Barb says you're in Seattle."

"Yes, just a short layover before I fly to Chicago."

"How was Alaska?"

"I miss you Stanley."

"I miss you too Danielle."

Then there was a long pause.

"My boyfriend bought me an engagement ring and asked me to marry him."

"Congratulations Danielle."

"I told him I couldn't marry him. He's a good friend Stanley. We've known each other since we were seven. We've gone steady since tenth grade, but I don't love him. When I flew up there, all I did is think about you."

Another long pause……..

"I LOVE YOU."

Stanley felt his heart pounding in his throat and his face flushed. The phone receiver in his right hand glistened with sweat.

"I love you too Danielle. I love you very much."

"Stanley…..They're boarding my plane now, I've got to go. I love you. Bye."

Stanley sat at his desk for ten minutes with his mind racing and his heart palpitating with joy.

"I have never been as happy as I am at this very moment," he scribbled on his desk calendar. It was August 23rd.

Then Stanley picked up his phone, wiped the sweat off and called Poor Joe's.

"Poor Joe's, Timothy speaking."

"Hi Timothy….Stanley here. I hear you have a bouncer to help Jimmy."

"Yeah, Jimmy's getting kinda old and I worry about him. Doug will fit right in, don't you think?"

"I do for a fact, Timothy. Now here's the reason I'm calling: Wendell and Chief are retiring and I think we should throw them the mother of all retirement parties."

"Mom's retiring?"

"Chief is your mother? I didn't know that!"

"Not many people do."

"This is going to be a very special occasion," Timothy said.

"Very special," Stanley replied.

Chapter 12

The Mother of All Parties

T he excitement was palpable at Big Bay General Hospital. Even a complete stranger could feel the vibrations pulsate through the walls and as it escaped from around the doors and windows. Chief was retiring and it was a high event.

For the younger members of the staff, Chief had come to Big Bay at about the same time that Jesus was born. As far as they were concerned, Chief demanded the same respect as a deity.

For the older members of the staff who had worked alongside Chief for years, it was a combined feeling of grief and joy. This event reminded each of them of their passing years.

Hospital business continued, but it seemed inconvenient. The Director of Nursing hired a nurse by the name of Carmen. She was a nurse of considerable experience and the nursing staff believed she would be Chief's replacement.

A special committee, named by the Director, worked on the details of the retirement party for Chief and Wendell. The committee members included Cap, Pete the orderly, Nancy Danielle, and from Poor Joe's, Timothy and Jonathon. The committee decided to hold the meetings at 10am to assure that Jonathon would be sober.

The menu included southern fried chicken (Chief's favorite), deviled eggs (a favorite of Wendell's), sweet-n-sour meatballs, Swedish meatballs, prime rib, as well as the usual menu fare, including Dora's red hot clam chowder.

Timothy mailed the invitations and many RSVPs returned. The Big Bay Chief of Police, whose name was Charley Johnson, called to say he would be pleased to attend. He had been with Chief in the French theater during WWII where he had served as ambulance driver and orderly. Rumors had it that Chief and Charley were once very close. Nancy believed they still were.

A member of the House of Representatives called from Washington D.C. to say he would be at the party. The Representative grew up in Big Bay. He was present with the pool players' consortium the very night Stanley announced he was changing his major from electrical engineering to nursing at Poor Joe's.

The residents at Poor Joe's actually remained reasonably sober as they cleaned, painted and de-cluttered in preparation for the big night. Doug and Jonathon pooled their money and purchased curtains for the old bare windows. The old bar took on a new persona, except for the stale beer odor embedded in the worn hardwood floor and the essence of tobacco oozing from the walls.

And then the big night arrived on Friday, October 13th.

Timothy and Danielle acted as the greeters at the front door. Stanley, Cap, Nancy, Crystal and the new nurse, Carmen, worked the buffet line. Dora carved the prime rib roast.

The laughter, the chatter and clanking of glasses in numerous toasts could be heard for a block around Poor Joe's. The old building trembled with excitement.

The Congressmen told a story of being treated by Chief in the ER as a child after being shot with a BB gun just above the left eye.

The Chief of Police told several war stories about Chief and himself.

"During one battle we got word that a French General had been wounded six miles west of our field hospital. We talked it over, and decided that I would drive the ambulance out and get the General. A Sergeant with a Thompson said he was going with me. Then Norma here, said she was going too and she out-ranked both of us, so off we went, driving around craters and through the smoke. About a mile from the front we hit a land mine and it flipped us over on the driver's side. The Sergeant had a jagged wound in his left thigh from some shrapnel that came up through the floor boards, but he was still able to move. Norma was in the back and not hurt. First we heard them talking. Then through the smoke we saw a group of German soldiers running towards us. I had a sidearm, and the Sergeant handed Norma his sidearm. We crawled out of the ambulance to a drainage ditch close by and started shooting. Our Sergeant was killed in that fight. Norma and I were trapped in that ditch all night. A French Battalion rescued us the next morning. I'll always remember spending that night in a French ditch with Chief. She is quite a woman!"

Chief Johnson told several other war stories, and then denied being Timothy's father and everybody laughed. Timothy stared at Chief Johnson for a few long seconds and then he laughed too.

The sound of thirteen Harley Motorcycles thundered as they pulled up in front of Poor Joe's. The peak fall color season in Big Bay had enticed the bikers from New York City back for a color tour. Having been involved in a fight with some college kids at Jen's Place downtown several years ago, the touring bikers now elected to find their evening refreshments at a residential bar.

"Sorry men, this is a private party tonight. If you come back tomorrow night the first round will be on the house," Timothy said as he blocked the doorway with his left arm.

"Well old man, we like private parties and we thank you for the invite." And with that, the burley biker boss pushed Timothy aside. Thirteen bikers wearing black leather jackets entered the retirement party.

Jimmy softly growled from behind the bar. The biker boss walked to the bar and leaned over, looking for the source of the warning sound. The letters on the back of his leather jacket read: HELL'S SPAWN.

Jonathon saw the jacket insignia first. "Hey.....!!! It's the New York retarded biker boys!" he screamed.

Chief stood up from her table of honor. All five foot, four inches of her marched over to the biker boss. Reaching up, she grabbed the man by his left ear lobe and turned his head towards the door.

"You get out of here right now, you and all your buddies, before you get hurt," Chief instructed the biker.

The Chief of Police reached into his jacket pocket which held his service revolver. Jonathon stood up, holding his wooden baseball bat as if he was standing at home plate waiting for a pitch.

In one fell swoop, the biker boss slapped Chief's grip away from his left ear lobe and with his right fist, knocked her to the floor.

There was no question about it; Doug had been drinking heavily. When the bikers first came through the front door, he had quietly gone upstairs to his room.

There is no sound like that of a pump shotgun being racked.

Now there he stood, halfway down the stairway on the west wall, wearing a Special Forces dress uniform, a green beret jauntily placed on his full head of shoulder length curly silver hair, and shiny cavalry dress boots. He twirled a 12 gauge pump shotgun over his head with his right hand like it was a baton.

"2,4,6,8........you idiots really want to participate?" he screamed down the staircase. His intense brown eyes twinkled with anticipation and there was no fear in them whatsoever. For a brief instant he peered up at the ceiling, and pointing up with his left hand, shook his head "no."

As Chief hit the floor, Jimmy was in flight, leaping over the counter towards the offender. Timothy frantically pushed his way through the crowd from the front door towards his unconscious mother. He had almost reached her when Doug fired the first shot.

Doug had loaded his twelve gauge with buckshot.

BOOM…ratchet… BOOM…ratchet…BOOM, and then BANG, as the Chief of Police shot a biker who had stabbed Wayne once with a Bowie knife and was about to do it again.

Nancy and Carmen screamed. Crystal hit one of the bikers over the head with a chair and he slumped to the floor, and Carmen kicked him in the groin for good measure. Glass from the east windows shattered and tinkled on the cement outside. Suddenly Poor Joe's was completely silent except for the moans coming from several wounded bikers and the sound of Jimmy growling as he wrestled with the biker boss on the floor. The front door dangled by one hinge now and made a squeaking sound as it moved in the wind. Jimmy had the biker by his bearded neck and would have killed him if Timothy had not pulled him off.

"His mother was a wolf," he sneered at the biker.

The dance floor at Poor Joe's quickly became an ER triage room. The physicians and nurses in attendance assumed their professional demeanor and began to sort out injuries by degree of seriousness. Three ambulances arrived within ten minutes. Chief was the first to be transported to the hospital. When she regained consciousness, Timothy had to restrain her from treating the others.

A caravan of autos transporting those with superficial injuries headed for the Big Bay ER.

Doug sat all alone on the steps that lead down from the apartments, holding the shotgun in his lap. Chief Johnson walked up the steps and sat down beside Doug and gently took the shotgun.

"You were protecting your friends Doug. Everything is going to be ok."

"Am I under arrest?" Doug asked.

"No Doug, you're not under arrest. We both did what needed to be done to protect our friends. Let's go down to the department and write up a report."

Wendell put his arm around Doug and they walked to the Chief of Police's car. Doug climbed into the front passenger seat. Wendell climbed into the back seat which is divided from the front by a cage. "I'm not leaving your side Doug."

"Thank you".

"You could see them again tonight, couldn't you?"

"I could feel 'um filling the room... told them they wouldn't be gathering any of my friends tonight Wendell...not tonight!"

Chief of Police Johnson listened to this conversation as he drove towards the police station and said nothing. The old war vet knew without asking.

Chief was treated in the ER for a 2 inch laceration on her forehead above her right eye. She refused to be admitted for observation. "My son will stay with me tonight," she told the ER staff, pointing at Timothy.

Chapter 13
The Embassy on Thong Nhat Boulevard

Timothy had been conceived in a French field hospital on a wooden gurney, which had resulted in his mother getting slivers in her butt. He was born to a single mother on February 2nd, 1945 in a London, England hospital.

His mother, Norma Bouvier, a Major in the United States Army Nursing Corps, was highly respected by all who knew her. Most people simply referred to her as "Chief."

First Lieutenant Sabrina Fife, who worked with Chief in the field hospitals during the French campaign, fell in love with the baby boy at first sight. These close friends discussed Norma's plight. One evening while sharing a bottle of contraband Bordeaux in Norma's room, Sabrina offered to adopt the baby. Together they named him Timothy.

Sabrina's husband was a Non-Commissioned Officer with the U.S. 10th Special Forces in Europe. Sergeant Major Dwight Fife was a force to be reckoned with. When he saw the love in Sabrina's eyes for this child, he filed the necessary paperwork and made a phone call to a General, assuring that the adoption was a done deal, and securing a promise that Norma was in no trouble. Baby Timothy was adopted.

At the end of the war, the Sergeant Major accepted an instructor position at The Citadel Military College. He moved his family to Charleston, South Carolina. They lived in a nice house on St. Margaret Street.

One day when he was seven years old, Timothy asked his mother why he didn't have any brothers or sisters.

"Well honey, Mommy can't have children," Sabrina blundered, instantly realizing the enormity of her statement. That evening Dwight and Sabrina explained to Timothy the circumstances of his birth and adoption, and that they both loved him at first sight.

"Someday, will I meet my mother?" Timothy asked. "I would like that."

He grew tall. By age seventeen Timothy stood six feet and one inch in height and weighed 190 pounds. He had a handsome face and Caribbean blue eyes that melted the hearts of young ladies when they gazed back at him. Timothy excelled in track. He became his High School's starting quarterback his sophomore year. Everyone loved Timothy.

After graduating, Timothy applied and was accepted entrance at The Citadel. He excelled in military planning and logistics. He became the starting quarterback for The Bulldogs beginning his freshman year. Timothy loved The Citadel.

Every once in a while, especially late at night after a few drinks, Timothy would wonder about his birth mother.

After graduation from The Citadel, Timothy, following in the tradition of his father, joined the United States Army. After boot camp, he applied for consideration to the Special Forces and was accepted.

Timothy became a Green Beret. Twenty-seven months later he was sent to South Vietnam.

Lieutenant Colonel Timothy Fife commanded an awesome group of young men. They found themselves involved in stealth operations in the

Mekong Delta and also in Cambodia as well as Laos. Several men were wounded, but no one died. Timothy received three wounds during a fire fight with North Vietnamese Regulars in an ambush along the Ho Chi Minh Trail. A medic treated him and applied field dressings over the wounds. He never sought further medical attention.

Chest x-rays done years later discovered a bullet lodged in the left 4th intercostal space next to his sternum just above his heart. When told of this, Timothy said, "I wondered why it ached during storms." He refused to have the bullet removed.

The war was going badly for the United States.

"We're being sent to the Embassy in Saigon," Timothy told his group. "The General has ordered additional forces for protection during an evacuation."

Marine helicopters were landing on the Embassy roof every 30 minutes and taking 30 passengers at a time away to the aircraft carrier Hancock. People were fighting and clawing up the Embassy wall trying to gain entrance as the Green Berets slowly drove through the throng on Dinh Chi Street in a M113 armored personnel carrier. They were waved through the front gate just as the sun set.

And then the crowds scattered as the Vietcong and North Vietnamese troops arrived in the area. The firefight outside the Embassy was constant with incoming small arms fire and B40 rockets and hand grenades. The Special Forces inside the compound repelled the first attack and then another and another as the helicopters continued to come and go.

Timothy was next to a Marine Lieutenant he did not know. Together they were operating a heavy 50 Cal machine gun trained at a hole the Vietcong had blown in the compound wall next to Thong Nhat Boulevard. Suddenly, a grenade flew over the wall and directly towards them. Like a seasoned center fielder for the New York Yankees, the Lieutenant leaped into the air from his crouched position and grabbed the grenade with his right hand. In a single motion he threw it back at the wall, just as it exploded.

The force of the concussion knocked both men to the ground.

Timothy had been partially protected by the large machine gun, with his injuries consisting of wounds in the right thigh and right bicep. The Lieutenant did not fare as well, and curled up in a fetal position, cursing.

"God-damn……..That one almost got us," the Lieutenant muttered.

"How bad?" Timothy asked, and he gently uncurled the Marine.

"Well shit…….sure looks like my hand is fucked," was the reply. And he held out his right hand, which was a bloody pulp, only the forefinger and thumb remained. He was also hit with shrapnel in both legs and on his back.

"Don't feel any hurt in my vital organs," the wounded lieutenant groaned, as he glared at his hand.

"MEDIC!" Timothy yelled over the roar of the war. "MEDIC NOW!"

"What's your name soldier?" Timothy asked.

"Wendell Jackson, First Lieutenant, sir. I sure could use a cigarette."

"Cigar do? Been saving these for a victory party."

"I'd love one sir."

Timothy lit the cigar and puffed on it several times. Then he placed it in Wendell's mouth.

First Lieutenant Wendell Jackson took a long drag and inhaled the cigar smoke just as a medic gave him a shot of morphine.

"Well fuck," Wendell said to all in attendance. "I'm a one handed wrench monkey."

"What?"

"I'm a mechanic……..have my own garage."

Timothy watched as the medic and a fellow Green Beret struggled up the ladder which was leaning against the Embassy tower that was being used as the copter landing pad, carrying a limp Wendell through the hail of bullets. Then the helicopter lifted from the pad and with the nose pointed slightly down, took off towards the east, flying just above the tree tops.

Dragging his limp right arm, Timothy crawled back to the 50 caliber. Grasping the machine gun with his left hand, he pulled himself to a sitting position. "God help him."

Chapter 14

Things Never Forgotten

Helen and Ira Weise left home and were driving up Wayne Hill in their blue Mercury Monterey en route to Benjamin's Seafood Restaurant which was located at the very top of the hill, overlooking all of Big Bay. They never made it.

The signal light was green for them at the intersection of Wayne and Mitchell streets. As the blue Mercury proceeded through the intersection, a dump truck filled with gravel drove through the red stop light and hit the Weise car on the driver's side.

Witnesses described it as a terrible crash.

The two vehicles seemed fused as they screeched towards the north, knocking over a light pole and then down an embankment together, rolling and rolling until they rested at the bottom with the dump truck on top of the Mercury.

Diesel fuel poured from the dump truck's ruptured fuel tank and down onto the firemen and rescue personnel as they crawled through the mangled wreckage. It took thirty minutes to free Ira and Helen from the twisted Mercury. The dump truck driver was able to free himself and refused any treatment.

The pungent odor of diesel fuel permeated all of the ER Department. Ira and Helen were drenched with it, as were all of those who had rescued them.

Ira struggled to breathe as he gurgled through the frothy blood in his lungs. He never regained consciousness following the accident and lived for about 90 minutes after arrival at the Big Bay ER. He died from head trauma and internal bleeding in Trauma Room One.

Helen's stretcher wheeled past Trauma Room One as she was taken to Trauma Room Three. Helen had been knocked out during the accident and was suffering from a concussion which she received when her head struck the passenger side window and then the dashboard as the car rolled over and over. She was conscious on arrival. After evaluation in the ER, Helen was admitted to the Step-Down Unit for observation.

"Stanley I need to talk to you."

Dr. Karen J Rink, a Family Practice Physician with an office located in downtown Big Bay, walked quickly to catch up with Stanley.

"Sure, what's up Karen?" Stanley replied, as they walked down the hallway towards Helen's private room.

"I've taken care of Helen for many years Stanley. She is terrified of men. When she was thirteen years old, she was in a German concentration camp. She had awful things happen to her in Auschwitz. When you go in her room be sure to have a female with you."

"Sure will, Karen."

And they entered Helen's room together.

"Dr. Rink!" exclaimed Helen, and then looking at Stanley with a confused and concerned look, "Doctor?"

"Hello Helen. My name is Stanley McMillen. I'm a nurse."

"You don't look like a nurse."

"I try not to," Stanley replied with a slight smile on his face. "Those hats make me look silly."

Helen stared at Stanley for what seemed to be a very long time in silence.

"I like him!" she said to Dr. Rink. "Stanley. I like him."

"I like you too. May I call you Helen?"

"Yes, you may call me Helen. Helen is my name after all. Please come back and we will visit when you have the time."

"Helen we have some very sad news for you," Dr. Rink continued.

"I already know," Helen said, looking at the two of them. "My Ira said goodbye and that he would be waiting when I come to join him."

"When did he do that?" asked Dr. Rink.

"When I was in the Emergency Room before I came to this room."

Astonished silence.

"We loved each other very much. My Ira was the only man I ever trusted. It will be wonderful when we're together again."

"Yes it will be Helen. Let's wait a bit on that, ok?" Stanley said gently.

"We'll see," Helen replied.

And then Stanley and Dr. Rink left the room and walked back towards the nurses' station.

"Wasn't that something!" Dr. Rink exclaimed. "And she likes you. What's up with that?"

Stanley was off for the weekend. Monday morning he stopped to check on Helen.

"I thought you forgot all about me," she exclaimed as Stanley walked into her room.

"I'm sorry. I should have told you that I was off for the weekend." And then with a big smile on his face, he continued, "I didn't think you would miss me."

"Well I did."

It was at that moment that Stanley spotted a tattoo on Helen's left arm. It was located on the palm side just above the wrist and extended up her arm towards the elbow.

"May I sit down?" Stanley asked.

Helen patted the bed sheets and said, "You sit right here."

Stanley sat down on the edge of Helen's bed.

"Do you mind if I look at your tattoo?'

Helen pulled her partially covered left arm out from under the bed sheets. On the underside of her left wrist was the Star of David. Extending up the arm was a series of numbers.

"My identification number at Auschwitz," Helen said, looking directly into Stanley's eyes. Her brown eyes were very sad from deep inside.

"Dr. Rink told me..........I'm very sorry this happened to you Helen."

"Would you like to hear what they did Stanley, the pigs, what they did to a thirteen year old girl?"

"Only if you want to tell me Helen."

"I have never told this to another man. Not even my Ira. I was afraid he would not have wanted me if he knew." And her voice trailed off to a whisper.

"I was thirteen years old and we lived in Berlin, my father and mother and two older brothers. My father was an engineer at the Mercedes auto factory."

"One day the soldiers came to our home and told us that we must go with them to the train station. They made us get into a cattle car Stanley—a cattle car that had manure in it.

"The soldiers told us we were going to a work camp in Oswiecim. It took three days to get to that place. The train stopped many times and more families were crowded in the cattle cars.

"And we had no place to go to the toilet Stanley. After the first time we did not care again".

"We got off the train and I never saw my mother or father or brothers after that."

"I cannot even begin to feel what you must have been going through," Stanley said. "You must have been heartbroken."

"I was mostly scared. I didn't know what happened to my family.

"And then they did experiments on me," Helen said as she pointed to her groin area.

"They did operations to keep me from having children. Then they laughed and wanted to see if the operations worked so the officers took turns having sex on me for months.

"I was thirteen years old Stanley.

"Then a General at the camp saw me one day and said I was beautiful and that I could be his housekeeper. I stayed in his place and he never made me have sex."

"The day the Russian soldiers came and rescued us was a wonderful day. I looked and looked and asked many people about my family. I never found any of my family. I think they had been gassed and buried in the trench."

Stanley sat on the edge of Helen's bed, looking at this forty-three year old black haired, brown eyed lady who had just lost her husband and who had scars beyond belief just barely hidden from view. Tears flowed from both eyes and he wiped them away using a napkin from Helen's bedside stand. And then Stanley dried his own eyes.

"I hate war," Stanley said as he held Helen's left hand. "And I hate bigotry even more," he added.

"I knew that about you Stanley, that day we met when Dr. Rink introduced us. I knew that about you. We have known each other for a very long time."

Chapter 15

The Worst Possible Diagnosis

The Director of Nursing walked quickly and caught up with Stanley. They walked down the long hallway together that lead to the conference room and the 7am critical care morning report.

"I want to talk to you after morning report Stan."

"Sure Ramona. Am I fired again?"

"You idiot."

The morning report took about forty-five minutes. Then Stanley and the Director of Nurses went to the Director's office and she closed the door.

"My mother died Saturday night Stan. I was by her side in her bedroom when she died."

"I'm so sorry Ramona. I didn't know she was ill."

"Mother was diagnosed with colon cancer about six months ago. It had already metastasized to her liver and lungs. Being a stubborn German, she would have no talk of chemotherapy. She said she planned on dying with her hair."

"I had no idea Ramona."

"That's because I didn't tell you Stan. I really have no need to share my burdens with others and that's not the reason we're talking now. I do appreciate knowing how much you care. I really do.

"I sat by mother every night for the last three weeks. I didn't want her to be alone when she died. I cannot think of anything lonelier than lying in a bed knowing you were about to die and to be all alone. When her bones started to hurt and bumps appeared on her skull, I knew she didn't have long. She had fevers and I would bathe her every morning before I left for work. The bedroom smelled sour from her night sweats. I have never felt so helpless. Dr. Silva gave me a prescription for morphine and I would give her some before I left for work and again several times during the night. My niece would stay with mother during the day while I was away. She's going to enter the nursing program next year.

"This whole thing has me thinking, Stan. I think we need a Hospice Unit here. I think we could transform the west wing on 3rd floor to a Hospice floor."

"I agree, I think that's a good idea."

"I want a Hospice wing, Stan. I'll talk to Lee (the hospital administrator), and the board of directors."

"Danielle went to school with a gal who is now the Head Nurse of a Hospice floor someplace in Boston," Stanley said. "I met her once when she was visiting on vacation. She seemed real nice."

"You and Danielle living together?"

"What does that have to do with the subject at hand?"

"Just trying to protect Danielle's sterling reputation, and to satisfy an old maid's curiosity."

"No Ramona, we're not living together."

"What's her name?"

"Who?"

"The Hospice Nurse in Boston."

"Jillena Avery, I think."

Richard Alan Hall

"Ask Danielle to call this Jillena and see if she would consider moving to Big Bay. Have Danielle call me. I imagine you'll see her tonight."

"You have quite an imagination. Danielle will call you in the morning."

Jillena loved Big Bay. She had vacationed there several times with her family as a child and had fond memories. When Danielle had moved from New Orleans to her condo in Big Bay, Jillena flew to the Big Easy. Together they took turns driving the U-Haul Truck 1307 miles with all of Danielle's earthly positions tucked inside. These two ladies were the best of friends.

There was nothing Jillena did not like about Big Bay. Those who knew Jillena felt the same appreciation of her. The boys at Poor Joe's would, given an opportunity, become a 24 hour body guard contingent. Several of the nurses at Big Bay General knew her, either from college or through Danielle, and loved to be in her company.

Jillena stood five feet, eight inches tall. Her dark shoulder length hair cascaded on either side of a face sculpted by a genetic heritage of Norwegian, French and Native American ancestors. Men considered her beautiful; so did the women. When she spoke, her intense blue eyes would never leave the face she was addressing.

Six weeks after the initial phone call, Jillena met with the Director of Nurses. Excited when offered the opportunity to set up and direct a Hospice Department at Big Bay, she said yes.

Work started immediately on the remodeling of the 3rd floor west wing. Two patient rooms were demolished to make room for a nursing station. Then ten private patient rooms for the Hospice Unit were constructed. It took six weeks, which coincided with Jillena's arrival.

The Hospice Unit became a success under the direction of Jillena. Filled to capacity most of the time, the unit often had a waiting list. The compassion shown and comfort afforded to their patients soon become widely known. The patients, and especially the patients' families, frequently

78

praised the hospice staff publicly. It pleased Jillena that her staff was receiving recognition for the love they were sharing.

Eight months after opening, things became very personal. Darlene, the Head Nurse for the Obstetrics Unit at Big Bay General, was admitted to the Hospice Unit with terminal ovarian cancer.

It is one thing to help a complete stranger through their sorrow and grief; however, these emotions are exponentially magnified when it is one of your own.

Compassion melts to anguish and deep agony.

Daughter to a Navy nurse and Navy fighter pilot stationed in Key West, Darlene grew up an island girl in every sense of the word. Her adventurous spirit loved the freedom of the island life. As a teenager, Darlene and two of her Cuban girlfriends started a business painting Caribbean designs on tee-shirts. They sold these tee-shirts to the tourists which crowded Mallory Square each evening to watch the sunset. Darlene saved most of the money and attended the University of Florida. After graduating at the top of her nursing class, Darlene went on to get a Masters in Nursing.

Her first job was as an ER nurse at Fisherman's Hospital in Marathon, 48 miles north of Key West. A1A is a busy highway, much of it only two lanes, and the only highway connecting the Keys to the mainland. It provided a steady source of trauma cases for the ER.

She also found romance. Eight months after meeting, Darlene married an ER physician. Two years later they had a son and they named him David, after Darlene's father.

The ninth year of their marriage was awful. Their son David was hit in the street while riding his bike and he died. Four months later her husband had an affair with a beautiful blond intern. The marriage was over.

Darlene's wonderful existence had imploded into depression. She had to leave her island life.

One lonely night she was looking through the classified section of RN magazine and noticed an ad for an OB nurse at Big Bay General, in the north country. *Now that would be a good change,* Darlene thought. The next morning she called the number and had a conversation with the Director of Nursing.

Two weeks later she flew to Big Bay. The Director of Nursing hired Darlene at the end of the interview.

When Darlene laughed, everyone around her felt the urge to laugh too; it was an infectious laugh. Her smile, while hiding a soul filled with pain, would light up a room. The twinkle in her dark brown eyes hinted of mischief. She loved to be outside. While living in Key West and then Marathon, Darlene would run for an hour each evening on the ocean beach.

She was loved and she was smart. Two years after moving to Big Bay, Darlene became the OB Head Nurse. She loved OB. It gave her amazing joy watching new life join the world, and somehow comforted her loneliness.

One warm fall evening, Danielle and Darlene were drinking red wine on Danielle's deck which looked down on Big Bay, as the sun set.

"I have a horrible back ache," Darlene said to Danielle.

"How long has this been going on?"

"Maybe six months or so; haven't been counting really. But now it keeps me up at night."

"Night sweats?"

"Sometimes."

"I've thought you looked tired lately."

"I am really tired Danielle. I have never been so tired in my life. I just thought it was from everything I've been through and being away from the Keys, but now I'm worried."

"Well honey, we're going to have this checked out tomorrow. I mean it."

"OK. I'm scared."

Danielle and Darlene held hands as the sun finished setting. Then they embraced and Darlene drove home.

Danielle picked up her phone and called Stanley.

"Hi, I need to see you tonight."

"Sure....what's up?"

"I need to be close to you Stan. I need to be with you tonight."

"If Ramona finds out, this will ruin your sterling reputation."

"I'm driving down to your place, honey. I'll see you in a few."

Danielle and Stanley sat on the couch in front of the fireplace as she recited her conversation with Darlene.

"I'm really worried. I think there's something really bad happening. She is so scared."

They talked for thirty minutes, and then Danielle stood up and led Stanley by his left hand to the bedroom. They curled up together in a fetal position and embraced for the entire night without saying another word.

It was a short night. The alarm went off at 6am.

"You are my knight in shining armor, honey," Danielle said to Stanley as she rolled over and faced him. "I love you very much. I cannot imagine life without you."

They slid closer and lightly kissed on the lips.

"I love you too........."

"We're gonna be late...!"

Danielle drove back up the hill to change her clothes. Both Stanley and Danielle arrived late for morning report.

The Director of Nursing had a smile on her face as they arrived, late.

Darlene underwent a series of x-rays and scans over the next two days, with Danielle at her side.

The diagnosis was the worst possible, a nightmare. Darlene had ovarian cancer with metastases. Her doctor told her she had just a few months to live as she squeezed Danielle's hand and sobbed.

Danielle called Jillena within minutes after hearing the test findings.

"Jillena this is Danielle. Darlene has metastatic ovarian cancer. Dr. Roosevelt thinks she just has a few months to live...." And her voice trailed off as she started to cry.

"Oh my, no; oh no, Danielle. This is just the worst! Poor Darlene; after everything she's been through. Whatever she needs....whatever we can do…damnit! The two friends sat quietly and listened to each other sob and sniffle over the phone, words failing to express the utter grief they were experiencing.

"I'll give you a call when I can talk," Danielle said after a few minutes, and they hung up.

A month later some of Darlene's friends met in the hospital cafeteria after morning report. Nancy and Carmen stayed over from the night shift and were joined at the corner table by Jillena and Danielle.

"Darlene has started chemo," Danielle said. "She said she knows it will not cure her, but hopes it'll put it in remission."

"I sure hope it works," added Carmen. "I talked to her on the phone last Saturday and she said she was tolerating the treatments ok…..just a little nausea was all."

"I just hate the thought of Darlene going home to her condo all alone every night," Nancy said. "She's all alone down there. She doesn't even have a pet."

"Before she got sick she would go for a run every evening and then go over to Poor Joe's to eat something and tease the boys," Jillena added. "Timothy told me yesterday that Darlene hasn't been at Poor Joe's in three weeks."

"Let's have a girl's night….a girl's night once a week," Danielle said.

"Yeah!" exclaimed Carmen. "Every Thursday."

"That'll get her out of the condo, and we can keep an eye on her," Nancy offered.

"Good Idea!" Danielle agreed. "Next Thursday at my place. If it's nice we can have it on the deck."

"She loves fish tacos," Nancy offered, "made with grouper. I'll call the Fish Market in the morning and place an order."

"She told me that her favorite dessert is key lime pie with real whipped cream," Jillena said. "I have a great recipe; I'll bring a key lime pie."

"I'll bring Darlene," Nancy said.

"It's a plan. Next Thursday on Danielle's deck....7pm!" Carmen exclaimed.

Designed by a world famous architect for a retired Warner Brothers movie executive, Danielle's father purchased this special place for his daughter when she moved north from New Orleans to Big Bay. The living room had French doors which opened onto a large deck that measured 20 feet wide by 30 feet in length. The deck was suspended over a steep hill rising up from Big Bay 800 feet below. On a clear night the entire city of Big Bay could be seen lit up in the valley below.

A Thursday evening with no wind, and with three natural gas heaters glowing overhead, the deck was cozy. Danielle lit candles and Jimmy Buffett sang "One Particular Harbour" on her sound system as Nancy and Darlene joined the group.

Darlene looked tired. Her athletic figure now looked cachectic.

"You guys!" she exclaimed, as she looked at the buffet, "My favorite."

"And Jillena made a key lime pie too," Danielle said.

"It's not from Key West, but I have real whipped cream," Jillena added.

Danielle served red wine and the dear friends chatted for hours. Darlene had a little wine and then switched to ginger ale. About halfway through the meal, Darlene suddenly stood up and ran to the end of the deck and, leaning over the railing, threw up everything she had eaten.

"I am so sorry...so sorry," she apologized as she wiped her mouth and chin with a napkin that Nancy handed her. "This chemo is kicking my butt."

"I think I would like some hot tea Danielle," Darlene continued, "Hot tea will go nicely with Jillena's key lime pie. Lots of whipped cream please."

The girl's night ended at 11:30. Danielle and Jillena had to work the day shift in the morning. Darlene told her friends that Ramona had granted her a medical leave of absence, and thought she would sleep in.

That night was the only girl's night that Darlene was able to attend.

Nausea and progressive weakness confined her. Her friends set up a schedule and visited Darlene every day. They would bring her warm meals and drive her to any appointments.

Over the next four months, Darlene lost 30 pounds. The constant pain became intolerable. At 1am on a Tuesday morning Darlene called Danielle.

"I can't take this pain anymore; will you drive me to the hospital please?"

Danielle drove her to the hospital, but first they drove all around the city of Big Bay. "I want to see it one more time," Darlene said as Danielle helped her into the front seat of the car.

The next day, at the end of her day shift in the ER, Danielle took the stairs to the third floor and the Hospice Unit.

"Do you know where Jillena is?" she asked the unit aide.

"I think she's in Room Eight with Darlene."

Danielle started to enter the room and then stopped, transfixed.

Jillena was sitting on Darlene's bed. The two friends were locked in an embrace and were rocking back and forth slowly in unison and crying.

Darlene moaned, "Ohooooooo.........ohooooooo......ohooo; I am so scared Jillena, so scared. I don't deserve this. I've been a kind person. This is so awful I can't believe this is really me Jillena. I don't. It's like watching a horror movie. God I hate my husband who left me for that little blond bitch, and left me all alone. And my sister, where is she? Damn her. Damnit! And my precious little David....I loved him so much and I miss him every single day Jillena, every day.

"I hate God," Darlene sobbed. "I hate Him. He took my little boy, my precious David when he was only eight years old."

"I'm so sorry," Jillena said. "Losing a child would rip my heart to pieces too."

"A car hit him when he was riding his bike." And then another series of sobs followed.

"I hate Him. Now I will never see my David in heaven."

A long pause ensued, interrupted only by sobs, as they continued to rock back and forth together.

"I have hated Him for so long.

"I wonder if He will forgive me…."

"Yes He will …..I know God will forgive you."

"How?"

"He has forgiven me many, many times Darlene. He loves us very much."

Another long pause followed, with only sobs and the sound of the bed springs.

"Please forgive me……..please forgive me…….please, please, please…….please help me," Darlene sobbed into Jillena's shoulder.

Jillena and Darlene looked into each other's eyes and then their foreheads touched.

"I will see my David soon," Darlene said softly between sobs.

"Yes you will; he is waiting to hug you," Jillena replied.

Danielle entered the room. Darlene and Jillena stood up. The three friends embraced for a long time in room number eight.

"I love you guys," Darlene whispered.

As the two friends walked together back to the nurses' station, Jillena asked, "Does Darlene have any family members alive? She hasn't had a single outside visitor."

Danielle replied, "Her father died several years ago and her mother is in an extended care facility with Alzheimer's. She told me that she has a younger sister who took off for Brazil with some guy, and hasn't been heard from since.

"We're her family now Jillena. Our love is her world."

Darlene lapsed into a coma that night.

When she died five days later, Danielle was holding her left hand and Jillena was holding her right hand. Nancy and Carmen stood beside her and the Director of Nursing was standing at the foot of the bed crying.

There was no funeral.

Danielle and Jillena took care of all the arrangements. Timothy from Poor Joe's called an old war buddy who had a private charter flight service and paid for two round trip flights to Miami. Quietly one morning, Danielle and Jillena flew to Miami and rented a car.

They drove down A1A until they reached Marathon. They drove past Fisherman's Hospital on the left and then up the Seven Mile Bridge. Halfway over the bridge they stopped next to a No Parking sign and together, sprinkled Darlene's ashes into the warm ocean waters that she loved.

Chapter 16

The Blond Cousin

P oor Joe's had been closed for three months following the havoc that ended the Mother of all Parties. Chief of Police Johnson called the State Police that night and asked for an independent investigation to extinguish all rumors of cover up, especially since he had participated. Yellow crime scene tape encircled the building for two weeks. Timothy and the inhabitants were forced to find housing elsewhere during the investigation.

Timothy and Jimmy, the guard dog, stayed in the upstairs bedroom in his mother's house. Doug and Jonathon stayed with Stanley at his house on Grant Street. Wayne, Morris and Ralph stayed with Wendell.

After the investigation was completed and the crime scene tape removed, restoration work started. The men entered their beloved bar and shuttered when they viewed the extensive damage. The large Schlitz Beer mirror behind the bar now lay in shiny little pieces on the hardwood floor and on the countertop, with little specks of dried blood on some of the shards. The 25 inch television above the bar had fallen to the floor and the picture tube had exploded. Buckshot had penetrated the juke box, causing an electrical short and small fire. The 45rpm records inside looked like little black potato chips. Much of the century old glass and window frames on the east wall at the entrance to Poor Joe's had been blown to tiny pieces by Doug's gunfire.

The worn old hardwood floor next to the juke box had buckshot holes. There was also a blood stain fourteen inches in diameter on the floor where the biker boss and Jimmy had fought.

Timothy and the fellows stared in disbelief. Jimmy walked over the dried blood and sniffed and then softly growled.

"I'm very sorry," Doug said quietly to Timothy. "I'm so sorry I did this to your bar."

"What the hell you talking about? You did exactly what you were hired to do Doug. You did exactly right my friend. Now come on fellas, let's get to work."

They dismantled broken things for a week. Stanley and Chief Johnson came over every evening to help. Doug cleaned up the shattered mirror. Jonathon and Ralph carried the broken chairs and tables to a big trash pile outside. Timothy and Pete scrubbed the blood stain with hydrogen peroxide and then bleach using a wire brush, but the stain persisted. Wayne and Wendell removed the window frames from the east wall and swept up the glass from the sidewalk outside. Chief of Police Johnson stopped by and helped Timothy remove the front door that was left hanging by one hinge, after the New York City "retarded biker boys" charged through it as Doug fired his 12 gauge shotgun.

"Good job everyone!" Timothy exclaimed after a week of hard work. "Now let's put Poor Joe's back together."

Ralph said he knew a guy by the name of Glen who owned an antique store in Traverse City, Michigan. Timothy called Glen, the proprietor of Rolling Hills Antiques, and discovered that Glen had a large vintage bar mirror with "Goebel Beer" printed in gold lettering. It was the perfect size.

Stanley found a business using the Yellow Pages located in New

Orleans that specialized in replacing antique glass. Timothy called and hired the company. They sent two men to Big Bay to restore the front windows.

While in search of a replacement juke box, Timothy found an old upright piano and thought to himself, *this will class up the place*; and purchased it rather than a juke box.

Timothy and Chief Johnson painted the floor late one night, putting a new coat of varnish on the hardwood floor with the buckshot holes and hint of a blood stain untouched. They finished at the front door. Then they walked out onto the patio together.

"Want a beer to cut the taste of varnish?" Timothy asked Chief Johnson.

"Sounds good. And maybe some chips."

Timothy went to the back door of Poor Joe's and unlocked the storage room. "Sorry the beer's going to be warm," he yelled back.

The two men sat at the picnic table on the patio, illuminated only by the corner street lamp, and listened to the crickets.

"Your mother and I were very close when we were serving in France together," Chief Johnson said to Timothy.

"She mentioned that."

"We were very good friends Timothy, very good.

"Did you know her when she was pregnant with me?"

There was a long, long pause.

"How did it happen that you ended up in Big Bay?" Chief Johnson asked.

"Well, I stayed in touch with Wendell......you know...the maintenance man who just retired with Mom. We served in Vietnam together and he saved my life. When he got out of Walter Reed we would write almost every month about what was happening in our lives. Wendell had to sell his auto mechanic garage over on Barlow Street because of his war injuries, and went to work at the hospital. I went to work as a detective for the City of St. Paul. I had been in St. Paul about a year when Wendell called me all excited and said a bar named Poor Joe's was for sale and it was more than I could resist. The rest is history. Moved to a town where I discovered my birth mother…go figure."

"Sabrina, my adoptive mom, and Norma were best friends in the Army," Timothy continued.

"They're still best friends," Chief added.

"Sabrina told mother that I was moving from St. Paul to Big Bay. I had no idea they had remained in contact all of these years.

"It took a couple of years, but one night she came into the bar all alone. I had no idea who she was, sitting there by herself in that last booth next to the stairs. When I announced last call, she just sat in that booth and stared at me. I walked over to her. She looked up at me and said 'Hello Timothy, I think we should meet. I gave birth to you in 1945.' I tell you Chief, I almost peed my pants at that moment. My knees felt soft and I thought I was going to cry, and then I did. I closed the bar and we talked until the sun came up. That tough little lady sobbed most of the night. So did I.

"She told me she never married, that there was no man who could hold a candle to my father."

"Norma did what she had to do at that point in her life, Timothy."

"The strong ones always do Chief; they just do what needs to be done."

"I can tell you this Timothy; she has carried a pain and emptiness in her soul even though she knew she was doing the right thing at the time."

"Were you ever married chief?"

"Never have, how about you Timothy?"

"Nope. Still hoping a very special lady will show up someday."

Then the men finished their beers and said goodnight.

The new windows were installed and Poor Joe's was ready to receive guests once again. Saturday evening at 7pm was the Grand Reopening.

Stanley and Danielle arrived after the festivities were well underway. The noise of the juke box had been replaced by the music of an upright piano. On the right side of the old upright piano stood a beautiful young lady, probably in her early twenties, with shoulder length blond hair, singing with a voice reminiscent of Billie Holiday.

"How in the world did you manage to get that kind of talent into a place like this?" Stanley asked Timothy.

"She's my cousin! She grew up in Nashville, but I never knew her growing up. Her name is Carla Fife. She just graduated from the Interlochen Arts Academy in Michigan and my mother, Sabrina, mentioned that she is an amazing singer. Sabrina called her and here she is; ain't she something!"

"Well I see who got the talents and looks in your family, Timothy."

"Remember, I'm adopted you idiot."

"Sorry."

"Have I got a story to tell you later.......later," Timothy replied.

Just then the piano player turned on his playing bench to acknowledge some applause. It was Jonathon.

"I didn't know Jonathon could play the piano," Stanley commented to Danielle and Timothy.

"No one did, but listen to him. He plays like Fats Waller!"

A wooden baseball bat rested in a green metal waste basket on the left side of the piano bench. Stanley walked over between songs and whispered in Jonathon's left ear, "What's with the baseball bat out here?"

"No one touches Carla. She's an angel from heaven."

Jonathon played and Carla sang many of the old blues standards. Then came requests for songs that Jonathon didn't know. After several declined requests, Carla sat down on the piano bench with Jonathon and whispered, "You just watch my lips......just watch my lips and play what you see. We can do this Jonathon; we can amaze the house tonight!"

For the next two hours Carla sang songs that Jonathon had never played before. He sat transfixed on his piano bench, staring at Carla's lips while his fingers played the music, and she sang every song facing him.

It had to happen of course. Too many hours of too much alcohol will lead to good ideas that aren't.

About twelve thirty, a man who had recently moved to Big Bay decided it was time to dance with Carla. He weighed in the neighborhood of three hundred pounds.

He approached Carla with arms outstretched and beckoned her to a dance. Jonathon stopped playing.

The big man patted Jonathon on the top of his head.

"You just keep on playing little fellow," he said. "You're bigger than a squirrel, but not by much," he continued, as he began to embrace Carla.

The sound was unmistakable, the low growl of a guard dog giving its only warning.

"One more move and he'll rip your balls off," Carla said softly to the big man. "Jimmy really will."

Drunk, but not that drunk, the big man slowly backed away from the piano. Pete, Timothy, Doug, and Stanley surrounded him.

"I don't need for this place to be closed on the grand reopening night," Timothy snarled at the big man. "Now get out and never come back....ever."

As the fat man waddled towards the front door, the sound of a trumpet being played came from the top of the stairs. Ralph had gone to his room and retrieved the trumpet used to play the national anthem every morning.

Together Jonathon and Carla and Ralph jammed until 2am when Timothy yelled, "Last call!"

The final song of the evening was Tin Roof Blues. Jonathon and Ralph played from their hearts and Carla sang the song facing Jonathon.

"Yes I love my baby
Well. I'm gonna tell you the reason why
Never told you this before
'cause there ain't a chance for a cut out
You've got to stay with me
Till the day I die."

Jonathon cried at the end of the song.

Chapter 17

An Arrogant Man

The week started poorly for Stanley. Danielle flew to Washington D.C. for a Critical Care Conference and Stanley missed her very much. And then there was the new Emergency Room physician, Dr. Gamal Nazar, who had just arrived from Egypt. The Doctor had attended the American University in Cairo for his undergraduate studies and then graduated with top honors from Al-Azhar Medical University.

An arrogant man, Dr. Nazar was especially demeaning towards women. When he walked into the room he expected all women present to stand and await his orders. When situations failed to go exactly as envisioned, the doctor would throw a temper tantrum fitting of a world class two year old.

Some of the nurses feared him. All of the nurses hated him. Given an opportunity, most of the nurses avoided working with him whenever they could.

Nancy, Sandi and Stanley were on duty along with Dr. Nazar when a farmer walked through the ER entrance with a towel wrapped around his right hand. Removing the towel revealed a large laceration on the palm of his right hand.

"Cut it on the bailer knife," is all he said, as he eyed Dr. Nazar.

Nancy and Sandi, in unison, gently shoved Stanley towards the farmer. "Your turn," they chuckled together.

Stanley positioned the farmer on the ER stretcher and cleansed the entire right hand with hydrogen peroxide and Betadine solution. The suture tray was undraped and prepared. Dr. Nazar entered the room.

"I have you now?" he asked Stanley.

"Yes sir."

The Doctor put on sterile gloves and demanded, "Needle driver."

Stanley slapped a needle driver with a suture needle locked in its jaws, trailing suture, into the doctor's waiting right hand.

The needle twisted to the side as Dr. Nazar tried to force it through the farmer's tough, callused skin.

Dr. Nazar uttered a foreign epitaph and in a backhand fashion, threw the needle driver with the needle still attached, at Stanley.

It hit Stanley in the middle of his forehead.

Years of boxing reflexes and instinct flashed. Both of Stanley's arms flew up in front of his face in a protective fashion just as his left jab headed directly towards the doctor's head at the speed of a snapping wet towel.

Stanley stopped the jab an inch from its mark. He lowered both of his arms and leaned in towards the doctor.

"That is the first and last time Doctor. The next time you throw something at me I will shove it where the sun doesn't shine."

"You have no idea who you are dealing with!" Dr. Nazar screamed.

"Yes I do; you are a nut."

"I will have you fired for insubordination."

"Well, be my guest.......Doctor."

"What an asshole," came from the farmer lying on the stretcher. "Get me a different doctor."

Dr. Nazar ripped off his sterile gloves, throwing them at the farmer, and stormed out of the room.

Stanley walked to the sink and looked in the mirror at the blood as it dripped from the tip of his nose.

"I sure hope you don't have anything contagious," he said to the farmer.

"I'm pure as the newly fallen snow," the farmer replied with a grin on his face.

Sandi wiped the blood from Stan's forehead with gauze and cleansed the laceration before closing the wound with steri-strips. "Sure am glad it didn't hit you in the eye," she commented.

"Me too! Pretty hard to damage a face like this."

Then Nancy assisted Dr. Wolf in suturing the farmer's laceration.

Stanley walked down to the Director of Nurses' office.

"Ramona, you are *not* going to believe this story."

"By the looks of your forehead, I just might."

Stanley relayed the incident.

"He has to go. There's a Board meeting tomorrow night," Ramona said. "Are you ok?"

"I am *so* glad I didn't hit him."

"Me too Stanley, it'll make it easier to fire his butt."

That evening Stanley decided to ease his loneliness and throbbing discomfort by going to Poor Joe's.

"Me and the boys heard all about that crazy doctor throwing a scalpel at you," Doug said, pointing to the steri-strips on Stanley's forehead.

"You did huh....who tattled?"

Timothy handed Stanley a tall glass filled with ice and Basil Hayden before he sat down with Jonathon. Then Timothy came out from behind the bar and joined the tenants of Poor Joe's at Jonathon's table. Pete, Wayne, and Doug, Morris, Ralph and Wendell all stared at Stanley's forehead.

"Yeah, we heard he said he was going to have you fired," blurted Jonathon, who was nervously fingering his baseball bat.

"Right... He's going to have me fired for him hitting me in the head with a needle driver….that *he* threw. Don't worry guys, honest."

"Why didn't you deck him Stanley? I'd have decked him Stan," Doug stammered. "Yes sir I would have."

"I believe you would have Doug. I'm sure of that; my money would have been on you, buddy."

"We all talked it over Stan. Us guys are going to pay a little visit. Ain't nobody gonna treat our friend like this or get him fired either," Morris proclaimed, peering at Stanley with his one eye.

"Now listen guys, this is nuts. I mean it. Stay away from Dr. Nazar. That could get me into a lot of trouble. I can handle this nut case. I've had practice, right Doug?"

Doug just grinned.

"I'll have one more Basil Hayden's for the pain and then I'm going to walk home. I mean it guys, do *not* get close to Dr. Nazar."

"Yeah, we promise Stanley," Wendell offered.

Thursday morning Stanley had returned to his office following morning report. There was a knock on the door. A very pale Egyptian physician walked through the door.

"I am here to say that I am sorry," blurted Dr. Nazar.

"I accept your apology."

"You have many friends in this city."

"Yes I do."

"Seven soldiers met me at my condo last evening as I returned from the hospital."

Oh no, here we go, Stan thought to himself.

Long pause…… "Soldiers; don't think I know any soldiers. What did they say?"

"The tall one said that you have saved many lives, but that I wouldn't be one of them if I ever threw another thing at you again."

"Well, sounds like the soldiers meant business, Doctor."

"And the Administrator has put me on a probation. He instructed me to apologize to you."

"Does that mean an end to your pediatric tantrums?" Stanly asked with a hint of distain.

"It is more of a burden than I had envisioned, living among the infidels."

Stanley looked up from his desk, staring at Dr. Nazar with bemused fire in his eyes.

"Come to think of it, maybe I do know those soldiers, Doctor, maybe I do."

"Thank you," sneered Dr. Nazar, as he turned and left Stanley's office.

* * *

Friday night was Dora's clam chowder night and Danielle was still in Washington D.C., so Stanley walked to Poor Joe's alone.

"How are things at the hospital?" asked Timothy from behind the bar.

"Things are fine....just fine at the hospital fellas."

"Well I bet they are, yes sir, I bet they are," slurred Jonathon from his corner table.

"By the way, is the National Guard in town this week?" Stanley queried.

"You know, I do recall they're on training maneuvers this month," Timothy commented with a slight smile on his face. "Sometimes they stop in for a drink when they're off duty."

"Yup. That's what I thought. Thanks for not hurting him guys."

"Welcome," Doug said as he climbed the stairs to his room.

Chapter 18

That Makes Us Not Really Cousins

"You and I aren't really cousins Timothy."

Carla was standing next to the piano, all 5 foot 10 inches of blond beauty with a soft smile in her blue eyes.

"You were adopted," she said with in a hint of southern accent in her voice. "That makes us not cousins."

"You and I know that Carla. The guys don't need to know. It'll keep things simpler," Timothy answered from the other side of the counter.

The bar had closed for the night. The conversation had interrupted his liquor inventory and cash register accounting.

"I need to order a couple more bottles of Basil Hayden's. Stanley goes through it when Danielle is out of town."

"I was thinking not simple would be nice Timothy. Kinda exciting actually."

Jimmy's tail wagged with anticipation as he watched Carla walk slowly towards Timothy, joining him behind the bar.

"I'm almost old enough to be your father …"

"Some of the guys think you're gay because you've never been married and because you don't date," Carla continued as Jimmy licked the popcorn salt from her left hand.

"Are you gay Timothy?"

Timothy turned and faced Carla. There was a twinkle in his blue eyes.

"That would be a 'no,' Carla. I'm not gay. I just have never found a lady that excited me since Saigon."

"What happened to her?"

"Her name was Thi Kim. She worked in her father's restaurant. I never saw her after the evacuation at the Embassy. She just disappeared. I never saw her again."

"I'm sorry that happened to you Timothy."

"Thanks Carla. It ripped a hole in my heart."

"Have you ever been to Mackinac Island?"

"Nope."

"Ever see the movie, Somewhere in Time?"

"I have not."

"It was filmed on Mackinac Island. I watched it in the theater when it came out and loved it!"

"Nope, I've never watched it. Starred that superman guy, didn't it?"

"Christopher Reeves," Carla replied. "Let's go watch it. I just bought it on VHS."

"Now?"

"Yes now, and bring a couple bottles of dry red wine. I have aged cheese and crackers at home."

"Jonathon will be heartbroken if he finds out Carla. He loves you."

"No Timothy, Jonathon doesn't love me. He's in awe of me and I think he's a very sweet man to look after me the way he does."

Timothy and Carla left Poor Joe's Bar in her robin egg blue Ford Mustang Fastback and drove up the hill overlooking Big Bay to Carla's condo.

Richard Alan hall

"How are you going to drive me down this hill after a bottle of wine?" Timothy asked.

"I'm not, Timothy."

Chapter 19

Armani Suits

A private jet landed at 9:10am Monday morning. It had been in flight from Cairo, Egypt all night. A long black Lincoln limousine drove up to the jet as it rolled to a stop. All of the automobile's glass was darkened except for the transparent driver's windows. Three Middle Eastern men departed the jet and climbed into the limo. They appeared tired after the 13 hour flight.

The Limousine then left the airport and drove to Big Bay General Hospital.

Doctor Lavern Smith had been chosen by his peers as the hospital's Medical Director three months previous. A kind and gentle man, Dr. Smith was much loved by his patients and held in high respect by his fellow physicians. This particular Monday morning, Dr. Smith's daily planner showed an appointment with Dr. Nazar for 11am.

At 11am sharp, Dr. Nazar appeared at Dr. Smith's office door. With him were 3 Egyptian men dressed in Armani suits.

"Hello Dr. Smith, may we come in?"

Dr. Smith looked up from the infectious disease report he was reading.

"Good Morning Dr. Nazar. Who are these gentlemen with you?"

"These are my brothers from Cairo."

"I'm sorry Gamal; the appointment is with you alone. Your brothers may wait for you in the lounge.

"There is nothing we will discuss here today that cannot be heard by my dear brothers."

"This meeting is with you, Dr. Nazar. Why are your brothers here?"

"To see that my honor is restored," snarled Dr. Nazar.

"Your honor?" Dr. Smith questioned.

"Yes my honor. You Americans do not understand the meaning of honor, I fear."

"Dr. Nazar, your brothers are not to enter this office. You may come in and close the door."

The 3 brothers retreated and Dr. Nazar walked towards Dr. Smith's desk. He did not sit down.

"I want that Stanley McMillen fired. I want that Ramona, the Director of Nursing fired. I want Lee, the Administrator, to present me with a letter of apology."

"Really? You want all those things, huh?" Dr. Smith retorted.

"Yes, and then my honor will be restored."

"Well Doctor, you were in the wrong. Stanley and Ramona will not be fired for your egregious act. And you can ask Lee for a letter of apology yourself. Good luck with that."

"You Americans have no sense of honor. I was demeaned by inferiors!" Dr. Nazar shouted at Dr. Smith.

"Well you certainly should know the meaning of demeaning. I hear reports from the nursing staff almost daily, Doctor."

"They are women and they are my subordinates," Dr. Nazar replied with contempt.

"I cannot believe the garbage spewing from your mouth, Dr. Nazar. These people are the wonderful human beings that make this hospital possible. Without our nurses, there would be no hospital. Have you ever considered that, Dr. Nazar?" Dr. Smith replied with disgust in his voice.

"So you will not honor my request?"

"I do not consider this a credible request. If there is nothing else, this meeting is ended."

"I will discuss this with my brothers. They will be very disappointed by your attitude."

And Dr. Nazar left the office and joined his brothers. They all left the hospital in the limousine.

Dr. Smith called Lee, Ramona and Stan to his office.

"Dr. Nazar was just here. He has three scary looking Egyptian men with him who he claims to be his brothers. He's demanding that you, Ramona, and you, Stan, be fired for insubordination and humiliating his honor. And you Lee, are to present him with an official letter of apology."

The office was completely silent for several minutes.

"What's our next move?" asked the Administrator.

"I really don't know Lee," replied Ramona.

"I think we should call Chief Johnson," Stanley interjected.

"We should," Dr. Smith replied, "but there was never a threat made, only ridiculous demands."

"We need some security. We need to hire some security for the hospital," Lee added.

"I know some fellows who can help us, I know just the men who can help," Stan commented.

"NO!" they said in unison.

"You know how they helped us at Chief's retirement party. They love us. They won't be intimidated by Egyptians wearing Armani suits."

"Those guys are drunks," retorted the Administrator.

"Those guys have experienced life that would make most of us drunks," Stan replied, "And they'll do anything for us, including staying sober for as long as necessary. They love us because we don't look down on their situation...I really respect those men, Lee."

Another long pause.........

"Ok, I'll talk to Chief Johnson," said Lee. "If he'll make those guys part of the police auxiliary, I'll hire them to get us through this mess, as long as they stay sober."

"Go talk to them Stan," Dr. Smith said.

That evening Stanley walked into an almost empty Poor Joe's. It's usually empty on Mondays.

"Fellas we need your help down at the hospital," Stanley said to the residents. He then told the men about the meeting that took place in Dr. Smith's office earlier that day and the subsequent meeting with the Hospital Administrator and Director of Nursing.

"I knew we should have taken care of that bastard back when we had a chance!" exclaimed Doug. "Back when he threw that scalpel and hit you."

"But you said, 'Oh don't hurt him. Be nice; please don't touch him.' Geez Stan, now look at the mess," Doug continued.

"Yeah, we should have," chimed in Jonathon as he fiddled with his baseball bat.

"Here's what we need. The hospital needs to hire some security men and the Administrator said he would hire you guys provided you remain sober and if Chief Johnson will swear you in as part of the police auxiliary.

"He will," came from the front door. Chief Johnson had entered for his nightly "nightcap" without notice and had been listening to the conversations.

"I will with two provisos. Number one: no guns. You hear me Doug? Number two: no alcohol while on duty, not even a bracer....right Jonathon?"

Then the Chief continued, "We have a real problem here men. I hope to God we don't have any trouble."

"They ain't gonna be here long enough to cause any problem," piped up Pete.

"Pete, no trouble. I mean it. Everyone understand?"

"Yup."

"Ok," Timothy said, "how about this. We have one guy at the hospital at all times, stationed right at the elevator by the stairs.

"I'll have a patrolman stationed in the ER twenty-four hours a day," added the Chief.

"And Doug will be assigned to be your driver Stanley, and Ralph assigned to Lee and Wayne to the Administrator. Dora can run this place; I will be Dr. Smith's driver."

"Those suits better not get close to Dr. Smith," Timothy said under his breath.

"Timothy, I mean it," admonished Chief Johnson.

"I will see that each of you has a radio to get help if there are any difficulties," added the Chief.

Stanley and the Chief left Poor Joe's together.

"This is a little scary having those suits in town Stanley."

"Tell me about it. The only people not scared are on the other side of that door."

"I sure as hell hope they behave themselves or we will both be out of a job."

"Probably right Chief," Stanley replied.

* * *

"Ok boys, this time we cannot mess up. Our friends need us for real now. They are in trouble," Timothy said sitting on the bar as Pete, Doug, Wayne, Ralph, Jonathon, and Wendell looked up at him.

"Where are they stayin'?" asked Wendell.

"Already checked when Stanley called me. They're at Nazar's condo."

"Nazar's condo," muttered Doug. "Nazar's condo...."

"I got to know some fellows in Armani suits when I was with the St. Paul Police department," Timothy said. "Stanley and the people at the hospital have no idea what they are up against."

"Will they hurt them?" asked Jonathon.

"I don't think so. They will intimidate them and frighten their families and friends until they quit and move away. Then Dr. Nazar will have his honor."

"Well let's just scare the hell out of 'em first!" Doug exclaimed.

"For these men, honor is more important than life. I don't think we can scare them away Doug."

These fellows I knew in St. Paul were in the import and retail business, mostly cheese, wine and olive oil. I saved the life of the wholesaler's son when the kid ran his Corvette into a tree after a night of festivities. I crawled into the burning wreck and pulled the kid out before the whole thing exploded....saved his son's life. His father told me if I should ever need anything...." And then Timothy's voice trailed off into silence.

It doesn't take long for news like this to spread though a hospital. It oozes through the very pores in the walls and through the little cracks. The nurses' aides seem to know first. Soon the hospital hotline buzzed. Big Bay General's staff quaked with fear. Many had been witness to Dr. Nazar's tantrums.

When the new security measures were put into place Thursday morning, all the fears were confirmed. Husbands and boyfriends drove their ladies to work and picked them up at the end of their shifts. They had guns in their cars and Chief Johnson told his patrolmen to ignore this fact.

Jonathon and Wendell rotated at the elevator bank, shifting roles between that of a Wal-Mart Greeter and that of a Secret Service Agent.

A Big Bay policeman was stationed in the ER; much of the time it was Chief Johnson.

The following Tuesday, the critical care morning conference started without the Director of Nursing present, which hardly ever happened.

The phone in the conference room rang and Danielle answered it.

"Stanley, the Administrator. He wants to talk to you."

"Chief Johnson, Dr. Smith and Ramona are gathered in my office. We'd like you to join us... now Stanley."

"I'll be right there."

Stanley walked into the Administrator's office. The Administrator leaned over his desk and handed Stanley a letter without saying a word. Stanley sat down in the chair next to the Chief of Police and read:

"I have pressing family emergencies in Cairo and must resign immediately." The letter was signed by Dr. Gamal Nazar.

"Do you have any idea what might have happened?" asked Chief Johnson.

"No sir, this is a complete surprise to me."

"You haven't heard anything through the rumor mill, anything from the boys at Poor Joe's?" asked Dr. Smith.

"Honest. I know nothing about this."

Chief Johnson continued, "The Lear jet flew out early this morning. The airport director told me that Dr. Nazar and those other three men were on board. He said they appeared to be in a rush to leave. No one had luggage."

"Stanley, just assure me you had nothing to do with this," said Ramona.

"I know exactly nothing Ramona."

"Something sure convinced them to leave in a hurry," Dr. Smith commented.

"Ok, well, let me know if anyone hears anything. Guess we can disband the security forces," said the Chief.

"I think they were getting a little thirsty," Ramona said with a smile.

Stanley was not able to sleep Tuesday night. At 11:30, he walked the seven blocks from Grant Street to Poor Joe's.

The bar was empty except for Jonathon sitting at his corner table drinking Black Label beer, and Ralph playing solitaire at the bar.

"He cheats," Jonathon slurred, pointing towards Ralph.

"How can you cheat at solitaire?" Stanley asked.

"He can do it."

"Where's Timothy?"

Ralph pointed towards the hallway that leads to the bathrooms.

Stanley started walking down the hallway and stopped. Timothy was talking on the payphone.

"Thank you…Thank you very much Vincent……You are welcome sir………I was just doing my job sir, but thank you………Thank you……You take care Vincent….Bye.

Timothy turned and saw Stanley staring at him. The two men stared into each other's eyes for a long moment.

"Just touching base with an old friend from my St. Paul days," Timothy said looking at Stanley without blinking.

"Thank you Timothy."

Timothy walked down the hall towards Stanley and slapped him on the back.

"Want some Basil?" asked Timothy.

"Definitely."

Chapter 20

Medic One

The Funeral Homes owned all of the ambulances in Big Bay. The ambulance attendants were the morticians and their assistants. Their medical training consisted of a basic Red Cross class and whatever medical knowledge that was gained in mortuary school. This sorry situation had resisted all efforts of change. Big Bay's mayor and his brother owned the funeral homes.

Early one Friday morning the final straw was loaded on the camel's back.

Stanley and Nancy were working the ER when the sheriff's department called saying an ambulance with John Brother, a prominent local businessman, complaining of chest discomfort and shortness of breath, should arrive shortly.

Mr. Brother had an extensive cardiac history under the care of Dr. McCaferty.

Stanley called the Coronary Care Unit to assure bed availability if needed. Then he called Dr. McCaferty and alerted him of Mr. Brother's eminent arrival.

The maroon colored Cadillac ambulance drove up to the ER entrance with both the driver and attendant in the front seats, with the siren wailing and lone red light on the roof circling.

As quickly as the vehicle stopped, Stanley opened the rear door. Mr. Brother lay on the stretcher with an oxygen mask covering his face. Both arms dangled down with his blue hands touching the ambulance floor. John Brother was dead.

"What the hell guys? You just put him in the back of your rig and left him to die all alone back there?"

"He was fine when we left his house. Just a little short of breath, so I put an oxygen mask on him," replied the ambulance attendant.

"Yeah, what else were we supposed to do?" added the driver.

"Exactly my point. Exactly my point guys."

That afternoon Stanley met with the Director of Nursing and the Hospital Administrator.

"You know, this is just nuts," Stanley said. "We have all of this life saving equipment in the hospital and have spent thousands of dollars training the staff, and we have yahoos loading critical patients into the back of ambulances and treating them with oxygen masks and bandages."

"Well, we've discussed this in past board meetings Stan. The medical staff has discussed it. The tradition seems to be entrenched," replied Lee, the Administrator.

"Good old boys, huh?"

"Now come on Stan. Do you have a solution?"

"Yes sir I do. I say we set up a rig with all the essentials like an ER room and we respond to critical calls."

"We don't have the money for that Stanley, or the staff," said the Director of Nursing.

"Here's what we can do, Ramona. I will staff the rig myself. I know Ralph Burritt down at Burritt's Dodge dealership. I bet he will donate a 4 wheel drive Ram Charger to the hospital. I think he would like the publicity and tax write-off."

Silence filled the room. Then Lee said, "If you can get a vehicle donated and if Ramona can spare you from her staff, and if you can get the Chief of Police to go along with this and help us with all the permits, you have my blessing Stan."

"Ramona?"

"Yes Stanley. Are you going to take this baby home with you at night?"

"Yes I am."

"Ok then. Stay sober at all times Stan. No Basil's."

"Damn….didn't think of that….ok."

That evening Stanley called Timothy at Poor Joe's.

"Timothy I need your help. You and Chief Charley Johnson seem close. When he comes in for his night-cap will you hint to him that I want to set up an Emergency Response Vehicle based at the hospital? Tell him it might save his life someday."

"Sure Stanley, I'll even give him one on the house. Oh wait, they're always on the house. I'll see what I can do."

"Tell him I'll stop by his office later in the week."

"Will do."

* * *

The Big Bay Police Department invested in all of the latest electronic communications equipment available. But on Chief Charles Johnson's desk sat three simple items: the first, an award for outstanding valor presented to him by F.B.I. Director, J. Edgar Hoover, the second, a candlestick phone, which he refused to part with, and still used, and third, a framed Purple Heart.

The Chief was talking on the phone when Stanley entered the office. He motioned for Stanley to sit in the chair next to his desk. When the phone conversation ended, he swiveled his chair towards Stanley and said, "Well, you've kicked the dog this time."

"Is it going to bite me?"

"No, I think I've put a muzzle on it. A good idea is a good idea. I just had to call in a few favors collected over the years. It'll be fine Stan."

"Thank you."

"You're welcome young man. I think we should call it MEDIC ONE."

"I like that a lot. Now we just need to get a vehicle."

"Taken care of. Talked to Burritt and he's eager to lend a hand. You just go down there and pick out what you need."

"You are an amazing man, Chief."

"Compromise young man... compromise. You go to the scene and do what you do best. The funeral home folks keep their ambulances for transport to the hospital. You ride in their ambulances if the patient needs you. Compromise."

"Thank you Chief."

"Just trying to help, young man. Good luck. Call me if there are any problems."

And MEDIC ONE was born.

* * *

No one goes to the hospital because they're feeling great. The complaints vary from minor injuries requiring a Band-Aid, to situations requiring life support.

On the other hand, when the Sheriff's Department called for Medic One, there was always a tragedy involved. The experiences associated with Medic One changed Stanley forever....

The forty three year old man had farmed since he finished high school. When he graduated, his father deeded 160 acres to him and gave him a John Deere tractor.

He thrived on the hard labor, and gained great satisfaction from looking back on his day's accomplishments. The smells of fresh earth and watching things grow gave this simple man a sense of contentment, even when prices dropped and money was scarce. He loved being a farmer. To help with the family budget, his wife sold eggs, cinnamon rolls and whole wheat bread at the farmers' market on Wednesdays and Saturdays. Together they had had three children, two girls and one boy.

He worked alone in the fields, saving a hired hand's salary which he couldn't afford, while waiting for his son to grow and join him. To accomplish the farm work alone, he had purchased equipment over the years that required just one person to operate.

It had been a bumper corn crop, and the farmer was chopping corn for silage. He had wagons equipped with a self-un-loading mechanism that fed the contents of the wagon into an augur that led to a conveyor which filled the silo. He had started working at 6am, chopping corn in the glow of the tractor's headlights. The weather forecast called for rain the following week, and he hoped to have the silos filled before foul weather moved in. As the sun was setting, he drove the John Deere and fully filled wagon next to the silo with one last load.

For some reason the self-feeding mechanism plugged. The tired farmer climbed up and into the wagon to kick the chopped corn loose above the augur...which was running.

He slipped.

The call came into the Sheriff's Department from the terrified farmer's wife. All she could manage on the telephone was a scream. "My husband is trapped in the silage wagon...oh...oh...oh my...hurry!"

The headlights on the John Deere were on and identified the location of the accident. As Medic One and an ambulance arrived, their headlights revealed a sight which haunted the rescuers for years.

The farmer's wife knelt under the silage wagon, her head just a few inches from the tractor's spinning PTO driveshaft, her hands and forearms covered with blood. She stared up at the blood dripping from the auger. She was awash in puddled blood which was coagulating in the dust.

On the farmhouse porch stood the couple's two daughters, ages seven and twelve, and their ten year old brother, terrified and crying.

A Sheriff's Deputy climbed into the tractor and turned it off. Stanley and a State Policeman climbed the ladder and jumped into the chopped corn and slid down until they reached the trapped farmer.

The spinning auger had snagged the farmer's coveralls and dragged his left leg into the mechanism, chewing it off at the groin. He was dead.

"I will never forget seeing his wife under the wagon, trying to catch his blood as it dripped down on her, and their children watching from the porch," Stanley told Danielle that night.

That was the very first Medic One call.

That fall was followed by a bitterly cold winter. Medic One had been called for several automobile accidents due to slippery roads, but nothing of note until an early morning call from an oil drilling rig.

The young man's name was Peter. He had run away from home at age fifteen and for the next six years traveled with a carnival where he worked putting up and taking down the various amusement rides.

At age twenty two, he met a man in a bar who worked on an oil rig. The job sounded exciting and the money was very lucrative. Peter quit the carnival and went to work for an oil exploration company.

He found the work more difficult than he had anticipated, and the hours longer. This particular night Peter was working the third shift. There had been a brief period of warm winter weather and tonight there was a freezing rain/snow mix falling on the men as they worked under the glare of the spotlights.

Peter guided the metal cable which leads to the top pulley of the oil derrick. The cable was being retrieved and coiled when suddenly Peter's leather glove caught on the ice covered cable. Peter shot up the derrick quickly, and his right arm was lodged into the large pulley located on the top of the rig.

The night foreman hit the emergency stop button with his fist, and then scrambled up the rig's ladder. Grabbing Peter's right arm with both hands, he went airborne as he pulled and fell to the platform below. Two rig workers climbed the icy rig and attempted to cut Peter's canvas sleeve and free his arm without success. The foreman attempted to reverse the cable and bring Peter down, but stopped almost immediately as the cable slid over the top of his arm, causing Peter to scream out in pain.

Peter dangled from the top of the oil derrick, hanging by his right arm in the glare of several spotlights as Medic One and other rescuers drove down the long two track road through the woods and up to the site. A fellow worker held on to the top of the ladder with his right hand and had his left arm around Peter, trying to support him.

"Need help up here! Help me get 'um down!" the worker yelled over the sound of the diesel engine. A Sheriff's Deputy and a crewman from the oil rig climbed up to Peter. Tools were carried up the ladder and the pulley yoke loosened until Peter's arm was coaxed free.

Peter came down the ladder slumped over the back of his fellow rig worker. He was conscious and in agony when Stanley climbed into the ambulance with him. Stanley started an IV in his left arm, and then cut the insulated canvas clothing away from Peter's right arm. The arm was nothing but mush. Stanley could find no pulse. There did not seem to be an intact bone anywhere in the entire arm.

"What's your name?"

"Peter, sir."

"Well Peter, that must have been quite a ride," Stanley commented.

"Yeah, would rather ride a Tilt-O-Whirl. How's my arm?"

"Not as pretty as your left one Peter."

"Good thing I'm left handed, huh?"

"I think so Peter. I'm going to give you some morphine now."

Peter lost his right arm that week. He lived.

The long bitter winter slowly merged into spring with its own set of problems, not the least of which were huge banks of fog which blew inland from Big Bay on a regular basis.

At 8pm on a warm spring evening, Stanley called Danielle.

"I really need to see you tonight, honey."

"I really need to see you too, honey. It's been a hard week."

"You haven't heard the worst of it Danielle. I just came back from an accident on Foggy Bottom Road. I'll be there shortly."

Danielle had a small glass of Basil ready and handed it to Stanley as he walked through her door. Stanley slumped on the couch and Danielle snuggled up to him with a glass of wine.

"What happened, Stan?" she asked

"A head-on just over the crest on Foggy Bottom. A couple driving a small foreign station wagon crossed over the centerline in the fog and were hit head-on by a logging truck.....one of those trucks with the front-end extending over the front wheels."

He took a deep breath and a sip of the Basil's.

"The entire car was crumpled under the truck. Just the rear bumper was showing. I went around to the driver's side of the truck and crawled under the cab. All I could see was a lady's right arm with a wristwatch hanging out the passenger window. I reached up and checked the radial... nothing. I wiggled in closer and sat up and shined my flashlight into the mangled metal. She had been decapitated Danielle...just sitting there with no head."

"Oh Stan.....oh man."

"By then a construction crane arrived and a cable was attached to the front of the logging truck.

"I lay under the truck as the crane slowly lifted the front end off the car. I had crawled around to the driver's door and was looking up into the wreck when I heard a thud, a thud like a watermelon falling off a picnic table and hitting the patio.

"Not more than fifteen inches in front of my face was a man's head."

"Oh God... how awful!"

"I can still see that head lying on the pavement Danielle. The smell of gasoline and diesel and a headless lady and a man's head lying on its left ear on the pavement and the sound of the crane's engine and police radios and the guys shouting to me and asking me questions.

"I crawled out from under the truck and rolled over on my back and looked up at the rescue guys.

"'Dead?' asked the Fire Chief.

"'Very, Chief;' I said. 'His head is lying on the pavement.'

"'Oh damn,' he said.

"I tell you what, honey; this has been a rough week. Real rough."

"I want you to stay here tonight, just stay here tonight and we can snuggle."

"Ramona is going to be disappointed," Stanley said with a little smile on his tired face.

"I think she would be disappointed if I let you be alone on a night like this."

* * *

Summer arrived all at once. The slow spring disappeared overnight and it was suddenly hot.

Mary was seventeen years old. Next year she would be a senior and then her plans were to attend the University of Michigan and to become a physician.

This summer, just as for the past two summers, she worked as a nanny for three children, ages eleven, nine, and six. Their wealthy parents owned a summer cottage on Big Bay, and would spend eight weeks of vacation each summer.

Even the shade from the giant oak trees around the cottage provided no relief on that blistering hot afternoon. All three kids were begging their nanny to take them to the public beach two miles down the road.

"We love the sand there….please. It's so hot out."

"Two hours after lunch. You know the rules"

Meanwhile, a retired couple drove towards town in their Chrysler Imperial.

Stanley took the call in his office. There had been an accident involving children on the street a quarter of a mile east of the public beach.

Medic One and Chief Johnson arrived at the same moment.

"She was looking around towards the back seat. It looked like she was talking to someone in the back seat... her car came right across the road and we hit," mourned the Imperial driver.

In the middle of the street a large black Chrysler Imperial had engulfed a blue Plymouth Duster.

On the highway, strewn among the metal debris, broken glass, and pools of engine oil, lay three young girls wearing swimming suits and the seventeen year old driver wearing a bikini and pink pullover.

Stan walked from child to child, kneeling down on his right knee and checking for any sign of life. Lastly he kneeled by the seventeen year old driver. And then he slumped to his knees and bowed his head with both fists on the pavement.

All of the children and their nanny were dead.

"I don't think I can keep on doing this. This heartbreak is taking a toll on me. Honest, I don't think I should keep this up," Stanley said, looking up at Danielle. He was lying on her couch with his head resting on her lap as she rubbed his forehead and right ear.

"Every time is hard when people are killed, but man, seeing all those kids dead and scattered on the street...."

"Life sure is fragile, Stan. We've known that for a long time; since we went into nursing we've seen this."

"I know...I know....it was just seeing all those kids. I want you to get rid of your Camaro, trade it in for something bigger."

"I'll do that when I have a husband who helps me pick it out."

Silence overtook the living room except for the tick-tocking of the grandfather clock.

"We need each other Stanley James McMillen. You were with me when Darlene was dying, and I'm with you tonight when your heart is aching. We love each other very much."

"Yes we do."

The following Thursday afternoon Stanley met with Chief Johnson in his office to discuss Medic One.

"Chief I don't think I can keep this going much longer. Between my job and Medic One, I'm worn out."

"I've been concerned Stan. Don't know how you've done it so well for this long. Almost a year now, huh?"

"Yes, almost a year."

"I was watching you at the accident last week. Everyone there could feel your heart breaking as you went from child to child."

"That was a bad one Chief. I guess the final straw, as they say."

"You might call it fortuitous Stan; this very subject came up at the commissions meeting last Tuesday night. Ralph Emerson wondered how much longer we could expect one person to provide what has proven to be a lifesaving service for our citizens. Jean Ackerson wondered how you have done it this long without so much as a day off. Everybody there agreed that we need an Advanced Emergency Medical Services Team for the city and county and there was a unanimous vote in favor of funding a trial program for one year. Then they'll put it to the voters. What do you think of that Stan?"

"That would be wonderful sir."

"And here....I have something they wanted me to present to you." And the Chief of Police handed Stanley a beautiful mahogany plaque with a brass plate that read:

IN APPRECIATION TO
Stanley James McMillen
(MEDIC–ONE)
For dedication to volunteerism and pioneering
of Paramedic Emergency Medicine in the Big Bay Area
We, the City and County Commissioners, thank you.

"Thank you Chief and thank the Commissioners for their kind words. It's wonderful that they see the value in what we did this year. It would have never happened if you hadn't stepped in."

"We did the right thing, Stan, and you proved it. Now, one more thing...."

"What?"

"Will you teach the EMT classes?"

"Yes sir. Yes I will."

CHAPTER 21

A Very Bad Day in Big Bay

R onnie had not injected any heroin for three days and every fiber in his body screamed. Tuesday May 12th was going to be a very bad day in the Big Bay General Emergency Room and a day of horror for the people of Big Bay.

For twenty minutes he sat on a bench in the foggy park across the street from the Willow Street Party Store, waiting for it to open. At 8:20am Ronnie left the park and walked towards the party store with a sawed-off pump twelve gauge shotgun under his long coat and a 38 cal. handgun in his waistband.

Seventeen years ago he was born to a single mother who became pregnant the very first time she had sex, on prom night. Married on three occasions to losers, as he grew up, Ronnie had witnessed his mom receiving years of abuse. At age seven when he tried to protect his mother from a beating she was receiving from her second husband, Ronnie was picked up by his right arm and slung across the room. One fall afternoon Ronnie returned home after school to see his mother's third husband slapping her around. Ronnie was fifteen. During the ensuing fight, Ronnie knocked the man out with a right hand punch. He stepped over the unconscious man, kicked him, kissed his sobbing mom on the forehead, and left the house, never to return.

He survived by selling a variety of street drugs and marijuana. Ronnie also used drugs to ease the loneliness in his heart.

He was addicted to heroin.

With his brain screaming for a fix, he burst through the front door of the Party Store and while pointing the shotgun at the clerk behind the counter, screamed, "Give me all the money and some Camels, and your car keys... bitch!"

The clerk's name was Sarah.

Sarah opened the cash register with trembling fingers. "Please don't hurt me mister. I have a baby girl."

"Shut your mouth. Give me the damn money!"

"Here!" And at the same time Sarah pushed the alarm button, located just under the counter below the cash register.

"Where's the Camels?"

"We don't carry Camels anymore. Sorry."

"Fuck you!"

And with that exclamation, Ronnie pulled the 38 cal. handgun from his waist band and shot Sarah once in the chest. The bullet hit her in the right breast and exited through her back.

The alarm rang at the Big Bay Police station and at Chief Johnson's home as well. Two patrol cars were dispatched to the Party Store alarm. The first patrol car arrived just as Sarah's rusty Ford Mustang was leaving the Party Store parking lot, the rear tires throwing gravel as it sped away. That patrolman radioed to the second patrol car and to Chief Johnson a description of the fleeing automobile.

Then he entered the store to find Sarah on the floor behind the counter, semiconscious and lying in blood. The patrolman lifted Sarah gently, rolled her to her left side and raised the bloody blouse to discover a large hole in her back that with each breath would suck air and blood and then exhale frothy bright red foam.

"Hollow point," he muttered.

Instinctively, this former Marine Medic covered the hole with his hand and called for an ambulance on his portable radio.

"My baby….my baby……my baby…," is all that Sarah gurgled.

Chief Johnson and the second patrol car chased the rusty Mustang.

"Oh God help me, please help me…..they're here," Ronnie cried as he navigated the narrow city streets at eighty miles per hour.

Looking in his rear-view mirror, Ronnie saw two alien space craft with flashing lights chasing him. They were being piloted by blue creatures.

Three blocks from Willow Street the Mustang ran a stop sign and hit a Volkswagen Bug on the passenger side. The Mustang continued traveling west, leaving a trail of radiator fluid. The patrol car stopped at the accident scene. Chief Johnson continued the pursuit.

Four blocks later the Mustang overheated and sputtered to a stop in front of Lisa's Meat Market. The driver's door opened and a young man with straggly dreadlocks climbed out with a sawed off shotgun in his left hand. He ran to the market door. The store had not opened for business yet. With the stock of the gun, Ronnie broke the glass of the front door, reached in, unlocked it, and entered.

"Damn…that's Ronnie!" Chief Johnson exclaimed to himself as he stopped his car behind the smoking Mustang.

Chief Johnson had known Ronnie since he was two years old. Fifteen years ago Ronnie's mother had moved to Big Bay following her first divorce. She worked as a secretary at Burritt's Dodge dealership.

"Ronnie…..damn it son, you get out here right now and talk to me. We can work this out Ronnie."

"Get the fuck out of here! I know you're one of them. Go away before I kill you too."

"Come on Ronnie. Put that damn shotgun on the floor and come talk to me… right now," Chief Johnson said calmly as he walked cautiously towards the shattered front door.

Ronnie opened the front door and without saying a word, pointed the shotgun at Chief Johnson.

He fired three shots.

The Chief was hit with two rounds of buckshot and then a slug.

Repeated attempts to contact him by radio went unanswered. The dispatcher at the Big Bay Police Department alerted the Sheriff's Department and State Police, giving them the Chief's last known location. Soon, five police vehicles converged on Lisa's Meat Market.

Chief Johnson was gravely wounded and unconscious. The first officer to arrive called for an ambulance. That officer crawled to Chief and dragged him back to safety behind his car as gunfire raged above them.

A tremendous gun fight had erupted. Six policemen, from the cover of their cars, fired their guns into the meat market. Ronnie fired his 12 gauge at the officers until the box of Winchester shotgun shells in his trench coat pocket was empty. He was reaching for his pistol when he was struck in the head and neck with a salvo of bullets. He fell face first to the floor and died.

The news had reached them. Stanley, Nancy, Danielle, Sandi, and Carmen from the night shift were gathered in the ER nursing station. The Director of Nursing was there too, as were three ER Physicians, Dr. Smith, and a surgeon.

"From what I've learned from the police dispatch, this sounds pretty bad," Danielle said. She was the ER charge nurse that day.

"This is the report they gave me. One young female shot in the chest at the Willow Street Party Store...sucking chest wound. Four college kids injured when a car involved in a police chase broadsided them; numerous injuries, none of which appear life threatening."

And then Danielle took a deep, deep breath.

Choking a little she continued, "Chief Johnson has been shot. The officers on the scene say that his condition is critical."

Fortunately, the Big Bay Emergency Medical Services had been implemented in April. All four of the new county ambulances were in use that dreadful morning.

The first ambulance arrived, bringing Sarah from the Party Store shooting. Her pupils were dilated. The EMTs intubated her en route to the hospital. An ER Doctor and Nancy and the on-call surgeon immediately went to work on her in ER Room Number One.

"Right hemo-thorax," muttered the surgeon. "Her trachea is shifted to the left."

The ER Doctor inserted a chest tube into the right pleural space and bright red blood gushed out.

"Oh man, that's at least three units," Nancy exclaimed, as she was hanging a bag of O negative blood.

"Guys... I think we should stop. Her pupils are fixed. She's not with us anymore," said the ER Doctor, after checking Sarah's eyes with his pencil light.

"I can't find a pulse," added Nancy. "Her rhythm is agonal," she continued, pointing at the cardiac monitor.

"OK, let's call it," sighed the surgeon. "Damn it!"

The second and third ambulances arrived from the accident scene. The Volkswagen Bug had been filled with four college students on their way to the university. The Mustang hit the rear engine compartment on the passenger side, causing the little car to spin three times before coming to rest against a large basswood tree. The students were shaken and bruised. None of them were seriously injured.

The first ambulance which had transported Sarah left the hospital with its lights and sirens on, headed to Lisa's Meat Market and the scene of the shooting. It passed the ambulance carrying Chief Johnson six blocks from the ER entrance.

"You guys are really screaming," the ambulance driver radioed to the incoming rig.

"Chief Johnson is really bad," was the reply on the radio.

Waiting at the Emergency Room entrance stood Stanley, Danielle, Ramona, Dr. Smith and the surgeon. They watched the ambulance approach at a high rate of speed and when it screeched to a stop in front of the ER door, Stanley opened the back doors and climbed in.

Chief Johnson had been intubated. Frothy blood undulated back and forth as the EMT bagged him. He was unconscious. Stanley felt for a carotid pulse and found a very weak, rapid pulsation. The cardiac monitor at the head of the stretcher showed a sinus tachycardia with a heart rate of 140.

"I've got a large bore needle in each arm. I've already given him two liters of saline. He's all shot up Stan," said the EMT.

Carefully, the group eased the stretcher out of the ambulance and into ER Room Two. Rapidly, the team cut away Chief's clothing and worked silently. Dr. Smith put in a left subclavian IV line as the team assessed the extent of the injuries.

There were numerous buckshot wounds in both his legs, the abdomen and left chest. Chief Johnson's right shoulder did not exist, being torn apart and partially blown away by the 12 gauge slug.

"We need to get him to the OR right now!" exclaimed the surgeon. "Let's get him upstairs and see what we can fix."

Chief Johnson was in the operating room for six hours. The hospital exhausted its entire supply of O positive blood (Chief's type) and then most of the O negative as well, during surgery. It became obvious that his injuries were overwhelming, and that he likely could not survive. He was transported by stretcher from the OR to ICU Room 4.

Chief's ICU room was filled with equipment. A ventilator breathed for him. He lay on a cooling blanket to reduce his oxygen needs. Four electronic IV pumps, two on either side of the bed, titrated intravenous fluids into his circulation. A respiratory therapist stood at the head of the bed, suctioning blood from Chief's endo-tracheal tube.

Nancy and Sandi worked tirelessly, changing IV fluids, starting additional units of blood and monitoring Chief's pressures and vital signs. Two Big Bay policemen stood just outside the door of Chief's room, watching. The ICU waiting room, packed with fellow officers from the Big Bay Police Department, Sheriff's Department and the State Police, radiated grief.

Stanley called Norma.

Like Moses parting the Red Sea, Norma walked through the crowd of uniforms and into the ICU with authority. A new nurse, who had been hired after Norma retired, tried to stop her as she approached Room 4.

"Sorry, you can't go in there," directed the young nurse.

Norma said nothing; it was the look from a United States Army Major that made the new nurse step back.

Norma entered the room and squeezed the hand of her only lover; it felt like refrigerated Jell-O. For a layman, the sight of Chief Charles Johnson would have been appalling. His body appeared swollen and puffy. His skin, now the color of a Vidalia onion, seemed almost translucent. Norma stared at him for several minutes, her jaw tight.

Nancy moved aside and Sandi put her arm around Norma's shoulders.

"We've loved each other for an awfully long time Sandi.... since France. And now I've lost him. You never really believe this day is going to come, especially after everything we've been through together.....but here it is Sandi....here it is."

Then Norma moved to the head of the bed and kissed her lover on the forehead. "I have always loved you Charles and I always will... I will tell Timothy."

And Norma left the ICU and drove to Poor Joe's.

Timothy was sweeping the floor when Norma walked in.

"Hello Mother."

"Timothy, your father has been shot and he is going to die."

"Dwight...what the hell happened?"

"No son, Chief Johnson is your father. He could never bring himself to tell you. Now I am. He was shot by a junkie over at Lisa's Meat Market. He's going to die today."

Timothy slumped down on a bar stool and looked up at his mother. Tears welled up in his eyes and his hands were trembling as he grasped his mother's hands.

"Oh Mother...oh no....shit!....son-of-a-bitch....I knew Mom, I knew and was afraid to ask him. Can you believe it? Two brave guys." And

Timothy took several deep breaths as tears trickled down his cheeks and dripped in the dust on the hardwood floor.

"Can I see him? Will they let me in?"

"Come on.....let's go."

Together, side by side, Norma and Timothy entered Chief's room. They stood hand in hand looking at Chief for several minutes. And then Timothy let go of Norma's hand and moved through the equipment and past the respiratory therapist to the head of the bed. He bent over and whispered into the Chief's left ear.

"Charles I have known you were my father since that night we varnished Poor Joe's floor together. I love you."

Chief of Police, Charles Johnson, died one hour later.

The funeral was huge. The Big Bay Methodist Church was filled to overflowing, and several hundred people stood outside the entrance.

Carla sang Charles Johnson's favorite hymn to close the funeral service.

"Amazing Grace, how sweet the sound,
That saved a wretch like me.
I once was lost but now I'm found.
Was blind but now I see.
Yea, when this flesh and heart shall fail,
And mortal life shall cease.
I shall possess within the veil,
A life of joy and peace.
When we've been there ten thousand years,
Bright shining as the sun.
We've no less days to sing God's praise
Than when we've first begun."

Tears flowed down Carla's cheeks as she sang.

Chief's best friends in life carried his casket from the church: Timothy, Stanley, Doug, Jonathon, Morris and Wayne, led by Norma.

Ralph played taps on his trumpet at the grave site, high on the bluffs overlooking Big Bay.

CHAPTER 22

Like Peeing on an Electric Fence

A blue funk best described Timothy since Charles' death. He couldn't shake the thought that this man who he had known since moving to Big Bay and grown close to over the years had died. The fact that Charles was his father and the two of them had never acknowledged it ripped a hole in his heart. The only other time Timothy had felt such heaviness in his chest was when he lost Thi Kim in Saigon.

He was sitting behind the bar staring out the front windows at the darkened street when Carla walked in. She had Mondays off and Timothy was surprised to see her. Except for Jonathon and Wendell, who were playing poker at Jonathon's table, Poor Joe's was empty.

"Hi Carla, what're you doing here?"

"I'm here to see you, Timothy. We need to talk."

"Oh... oh," came in unison from the southwest table.

"You quitting?" asked Timothy.

"Give me a break That's what I'm talking about. You are *way* down in the dumps. Let's go for a walk."

Timothy looked up from his stool, his blue eyes clouded with agony. "Ok. You guys look after the bar."

Carla took his hand and led him out the front door. Jimmy followed them as they walked down a dark Union Street, illuminated only by an occasional street light.

"Timothy, we need to get out of Dodge."

"We do huh?"

"Yes. We need to get far away from here and eat good food and drink good wine and fool-around. Not necessarily in that order."

"I don't think I could stand another bit of pain in my life Carla. I think if I get closer to you and then lose you I would just curl up in a corner and let myself die."

"TIMOTHY.........I love you. You've become the most important thing in my life. All day long I find my mind drifting to you and wondering what you're doing and wishing I could be with you."

They came to a park bench and sat down.

"Whew!" Timothy uttered.

"I mean it! I'm in love with you. And every time you look at me I see that love shining in your soul for me."

"Carla, you are the most amazing person I've ever met. I love you too."

After a deep breath, Timothy continued, "I am not the BIG BRAVE SPECIAL FORCES DECORATED FEARLESS LIEUTENANT COLONEL that the world thinks it knows. I wasn't even brave enough to talk with Charles man to man. My heart aches and my soul is crying. I have been afraid since I lost Thi Kim... I'm not afraid of death," and he took another deep breath... "I am afraid of losing those around me Carla."

"You are not going to lose me. I was sent here to be by your side...I really believe this Timothy, YOU ARE THE ONE," she said empathetically, looking directly into his eyes.

"When I was attending the Interlochen Arts Academy in Michigan we would go to Traverse City on Saturday nights. It's a beautiful little city right on Lake Michigan with lots of great restaurants and night life. Let's fly there, and then after a couple of days we can rent a car and drive up to Mackinaw City and take a ferry to Mackinac Island and spend a week."

"I've got a bar to run Carla."

"Wendell would love to cover for you. Between Wendell and Dora, the place'll be just fine without you for a couple of weeks. Besides, to be quite frank, people are staying away right now because they can't stand to see you this way."

"Really?"

"Yes…really. And you'll come back a changed man. That much I promise you ….a changed man."

"Carla..."

"Yes..."

"Thank you."

Five days later a Northwest Airlines plane landed at the Cherry Capital Airport in Traverse City. A cab drove them to the Park Place Hotel on State Street in the downtown district.

Carla had reserved a room on the tenth floor in the historic tower which overlooked West Grand Traverse Bay and downtown Traverse City. The sun had set by the time they were checked in and arrived in their room.

"You weren't kidding Carla," Timothy said as he gazed out the window. "This is beautiful."

"Let's get unpacked and freshened up and then go downtown. I made us reservations at Amical. You'll love it!"

Hand in hand, Timothy and Carla walked west on Front Street until they reached the restaurant known as Amical. The smells of French cuisine leaked out the front door each time it was opened. They were seated outside under the covered patio, facing Front Street. The evening was cool, but the overhead gas heaters made the patio tropically warm. Watching the pedestrians walking by on the other side of the wrought-iron fence as they shared French onion soup and olive twists, Timothy became visibly relaxed. As they ate their leisurely meal, Carla could see the sparkle slowly returning to Timothy's eyes. After dinner, he ordered his third adult beverage of the evening.

"I believe I'll have a Basil Hayden's," Timothy proclaimed to the waiter. "Stanley swears by Basil's," he added with a smile on his face. It was the first smile Carla had seen on his face since Chief Johnson's death.

They crossed Front Street and were heading back to the hotel when they heard the music.

"This place is new since I was here last," Carla commented.

The sign above the door read, "PHIL's on Front. Restaurant and Chocolate Bar."

"Let's go in and listen....and get some dessert!"

They found two seats at the bar just a few feet away from the bandstand.

"What are their names?" Carla asked the bartender as she nodded to the keyboarder and vocalist.

"The singer's name is Miriam Pico, and the man on the keyboards is David Chown. They've recorded at least three CDs together that I know of," the bartender replied.

"They're really good Carla.....I mean world class good," Timothy exclaimed.

Miriam sang a song titled, "I Will Love You Anyway," and then "In the Heart of Another." Then she sang a song written by Van Morrison, "Tupelo Honey":

"You can't stop us on the road to freedom.
You can't keep us cause our eyes can see.
She's as sweet as tupelo honey.
She's an angel of the first degree.
She's as sweet as tupelo honey.
Just like honey from the bee."

Timothy watched Carla enjoy the music. For a moment he thought he might start crying.

At the end of the final set, Timothy left in search of the Men's Room. Carla walked up to the bandstand and introduced herself to Miriam and David.

"Will you guys play at our wedding?" she asked.

"We love playing at weddings," Miriam replied and David nodded in the affirmative.

Miriam handed Carla a card with contact information.

"I want you to sing at our wedding. We live in Big Bay. I'll pay all your travel expenses. Having you two will make this a very special occasion. I'm so happy we heard you tonight."

"Let us know the date so we can schedule it," David said.

"I will as soon as he asks me," Carl replied, pointing towards Timothy as he returned from the Men's Room.

For three days Carla and Timothy played in Traverse City. By the end of the third day Carla sensed Timothy's agony being erased by happiness and she knew it was her love that was healing the rip in his heart.

Then they drove a rented car to Mackinaw City and took a Starline Ferry to Mackinac Island. Carla had made reservations at The Grand Hotel for the next seven days.

After the horse drawn carriage ride to the hotel, they walked up the long, long porch that looks down on the city and out at the majestic Mackinac Bridge.

"This is one of the most beautiful places I've ever seen, Carla," Timothy said, as they sat side by side in wooden rocking chairs on the eight hundred and eighty foot long covered porch, looking out at the mighty Mackinac Bridge. They sat side by side for over an hour, watching the horse drawn carriages bringing guests from the docks. In the distance they could see the ferries scooting back and forth between Mackinaw City and the island. From Huron Street down below drifted the happy sounds of tourists spending money, and the sound of a band playing at Horn's Bar.

They went to their room and as they unpacked the suitcases Timothy exclaimed, "This is just like the movie we watched together that first night in your condo Carla….just like the movie!"

"Told you!"

And then suddenly Carla grasped Timothy by the shoulders, spun him around and pushed him flat on the bed, pinning his shoulders with her hands and his torso with her body.

Looking up, Timothy saw a beautiful lady staring down with immense love in her blue eyes. Her soft long blond hair came over her shoulders and tickled his face.

"It's been eleven months, twenty days and seven hours since I first walked into Poor Joe's Bar and laid eyes on you Timothy Fife I said to myself at that moment, 'Carla Fife, someday that man is going to be your husband.'"

Timothy trembled.

He closed his eyes as he felt the poisons of pain and sorrow being drawn from his soul by this loving creature and being replaced with the glorious warmth of love. The incredulous feeling sparked his memory of the time when, as a little fellow, he had taken a dare to pee on an electric fence. Carla's hands were drawing the pulsating agony right out of his body.

"Timothy…..I love you."

Timothy opened his eyes, which were now filled with tears.

"I love you Carla. I love you …. I love you …..I love you. You are the most amazing person I have ever met."

"Mutual admiration society," Carla replied.

And with that Timothy lifted Carla above his head like a weight-lifter doing bench presses.

"Will you marry me Carla?" Timothy asked, looking up at her.

"Yes I will! I will love being your wife. I have waited my entire life for you."

Timothy put Carla on the bed beside him. Then he walked to the closet and took a small box out of his jacket pocket.

Carla was sitting on the edge of the bed when Timothy turned around. He walked back to her and went down on one knee as he opened the box.

Staring down into that simple small leather box, Carla saw a beautiful chocolate diamond solitaire engagement ring. She had never seen anything like that ring in her life.

"Timothy! "When did you get this?"

"The Tuesday after we went for a walk and you said we needed to get out of Dodge."

"Oh…it's beautiful!"

"I've been waiting my whole life… waiting for you. Here….let's put it on. Todd down at Diamond Jewelers knew your size. He said you are his favorite customer!"

The ring fit perfectly. Carla sat on the edge of the bed and wept with joy.

"A perfect fit, just like us."

For several minutes they looked out the window of their hotel room and held each other tightly.

"We should get dressed for dinner; I made reservations at The Woods restaurant for eight. The carriage will pick us up in front of the hotel at seven thirty."

The horse drawn carriage ride from The Grand Hotel to The Woods restaurant on the other side of Mackinac Island took twenty minutes. Timothy had his arm around Carla the entire ride. Carla alternated gazing at her engagement ring and the face of the man she adored.

They were seated at a secluded table in the rustic old restaurant. Together they shared a bottle of rare Chalone Pinot Noir. Carla chose chilled cucumber and honeydew soup followed by salmon steak wrapped in smoked bacon. Timothy ordered Austrian steak soup followed by hazelnut crusted venison. Together at this secluded table they felt complete contentment. Timothy's empty spot, which he long ago accepted, had been filled. He loved this completely foreign feeling. Carla sat across from the man she knew would be her lover for the rest of her life. She had never felt the joy she experienced with this man.

It was almost midnight. A carriage was waiting as they walked out of the restaurant for the ride back to The Grand. The island air had a Lake Huron chill and Carla snuggled close to Timothy as the carriage headed down the dark road with bright stars shining overhead. As they passed under the canopy of oak and birch trees, she turned her head and lightly kissed Timothy on his cheek. The faint smell of Old Spice lingered and she inhaled deeply. Carla had grown fond of Old Spice.

As they neared The Grand, Carla instructed the driver to bypass the hotel and to travel down the hill to The Mustang Lounge.

"This is where the locals hang out. Come on, this is going to be fun," she said with a huge grin on her face as she lead Timothy up the wooden steps.

"Lieutenant Colonel Timothy Fife. Well I'll be god damned!" screamed the nearly toothless bartender.

Timothy stopped just inside the screen door and stared.

"Be right back," he whispered to Carla. Then with the agility of a younger man, Timothy leapt over the bar and picked the bartender up in a bear hug.

"Gary, you old sonofabitch! Look at you. You don't look a day over one hundred," Timothy proclaimed.

And then Timothy turned the man to face Carla and the assembled patrons.

"This Green Beret was in Saigon with me when we were evacuating the Embassy in 1975. The last time I saw this soldier he was climbing a ladder to the copter pad with a wounded marine on his back while the Viet Cong were trying to shoot him. Man, look at you. I'm so happy to see you again."

"I'm glad to see you too, Colonel. Do you know what ever happened to that marine we evacuated to the carrier?"

"Yes sir, he's running my bar back in Big Bay right now. His name is Wendell. He's doing just fine. You guys should have a reunion!"

"Damn right we will! Next round is on the house everyone. To old times and friends forever," announced Gary.

"Everybody, I want to introduce my fiancé and most amazing human being, Carla Fife."

And Carla raised her left hand to show the assembled admirers her engagement ring.

Gary leaned into Timothy and asked, "Same last name?

"Yup, cousins can marry in Big Bay, Gary."

"Oh."

The festivities continued until 2am when The Mustang closed. Timothy and Carla walked up the hill towards The Grand Hotel, hand in hand and happy.

"You are a magic lady," Timothy said. "How did you do that thing on the bed this afternoon? I could feel all the sadness being drawn right out of my body. How did you do that?"

"That is what love can do Timothy," Carla replied. "That's the power of love. I am your missing link."

"Remarkable!"

Chapter 23

A Mouth That Could Not Lie

Happy people filled Poor Joe's. During a late night phone conversation, Carla excitedly told Danielle the news of the engagement. When Timothy and Carla returned to Big Bay and Poor Joe's, their friends planned an evening of welcoming festivities.

"Timothy must be all better if he proposed to Carla," Jonathon proclaimed to the assembled as he played the piano.

"You betcha," agreed Ralph as he cleaned the spit out of his trumpet.

The young lady stood 5 foot 6 inches tall. With green eyes that sparkled, black hair pulled back into a ponytail and a perpetual smile on her slender face, her presence could not be ignored. She greeted Timothy and Carla as they entered Poor Joe's.

"I'm sorry sir; all of our available tables are taken. There's a little standing room up at the bar. If you give me your name, I'll find you if a table is cleared. We've got a big event here tonight!"

"What's your name dear?" Timothy asked.

"Heather. I'm the new hostess here," she explained with a giant grin on her pretty face.

"You are? Well congratulations Heather. Who hired you?"

"The boss man, right over there." Heather was pointing at Wendell.

"What's your name?" Heather asked.

"Timothy Fife."

"Oooooh... oh! Hey everyone... LOOK WHO'S HERE!" Heather yelled over the sound of laughter and the piano.

Jonathon stopped playing in mid note. A roar went up that shook the windows and could be heard for a block in all directions.

Pete, Morris, Wayne and Ralph grabbed Timothy and hoisted him over their heads. They carried him horizontally to a reserved table of honor. Danielle, Carmen, Nancy, Norma, Jillena and Jonathon swarmed around Carla and escorted her to the table.

"I love you Carla....and your ring is so pretty. I'm very happy for you and Timothy," Jonathon stammered as they pushed through the crowd to the designated table.

"I love you too Jonathon. You are a most wonderful friend to me."

"Hey Wendell, come here!" Timothy yelled.

"Welcome home Timothy. Man you look a lot better than when you left."

"I feel like a new man. Now, who the hell is Heather and what is she doing here?"

"Let me get you a drink first.....Dr. Daniels?"

"Nope, switched to Basil's."

Timothy took a long sip of the Basil's and over the rim of the glass saw Stanley smiling down at him.

"Good to see you back in form Timothy."

"Great to be back in form Stan...Wendell...."

"Well you see," stated Wendell, "Stanley took care of her baby in the ER and she needed a job 'cuz she's a single mom and we needed more help since Dora started with the new menu and so here she is. How'd I do?"

"You're kidding right? And a new menu?"

"Just talk to her, Timothy," Stanley said. "Just ask her about the menu or something and you'll see. She's special."

"Hey Heather, will you please bring me one of those new menus?" Timothy yelled over the din.

Heather pushed through the crowd, waving the menu high above her head.

"Here you are sir."

"White Chicken Chili, Boaster Chicken, Killer Texan Chili, Sirloin Steak Sandwiches, Delicious Buffalo Burgers, Soup of the Day. Holy shit, Wendell! Where do you keep all this stuff?"

"In the beer cooler."

"Ok, Heather, which one of these new deserts is your favorite?" Timothy asked, looking at the back of the new menu.

"We don't have most of them yet sir, but aren't they pretty?"

"Ok, what about this page? What's good?" he asked, looking at the front.

"Well it's all good except for the Killer Chili. My mouth can't tell a lie; it's not so good sir."

"Well welcome to Poor Joe's Heather. Call me Timothy. Where are you staying with your baby?"

Heather pointed upstairs and shrugged.

Carla leaned over the table and took Heather by the hand.

"Honey, you and your baby can stay with me until things are all sorted out. Do you have a baby boy or girl?"

"Boy. His name is Justice. He's six months old."

"Well you and Justice just come and stay with me. Where is Justice right now?"

"Doug has him. Doug and him are together lots. Doug is very kind to us."

"Oh, by the way Wendell, Carla and I ran into a Green Beret who was bartending at The Mustang Lounge on Mackinac Island. We were all at the Embassy together during the evacuation."

"Who?"

"Lieutenant Gary Jamison."

"Don't remember him."

"He's the soldier who carried you on his back up the ladder to the copter pad and went with you to the carrier."

"I don't remember. Got to meet him."

"You will. He's coming to the wedding."

CHAPTER 24

Sweet as Tupelo Honey

C arla and Timothy planned their wedding for October 10th. Gary Jamison took the ferry from Mackinac Island to Mackinaw City. Then he drove to the Pellston airport and flew to Big Bay. Sabrina and Dwight Fife flew in from Charleston. A Marine Honor Guard arrived on a large green bus from Camp Lejeune. Miriam Pico and David Chown flew from Traverse City to Big Bay with their musical instruments.

Norma was waiting for Sabrina and Dwight at the airport. Sabrina pushed Dwight through the airport lobby in a wheelchair and together they helped him into the front seat of Norma's Mercedes. Before they climbed into the car, Sabrina and Norma hugged for several minutes.

"Our little boy is all grown up and getting married," Norma whispered in Sabrina's left ear.

"I'm so happy for him Norma. See, everything turned out fine, just like I promised."

"Yes you did. I love you Sabrina. Thank you for…." And Norma's voice choked.

They got in the car and Norma drove towards the Red Oaks Hotel.

"You look like hell," Dwight said, looking at Norma.

"Well you look just great Dwight, not a day over 96 I'd say," Norma retorted.

"You've lost weight Norma," Sabrina added from the back seat.

"Weight Watchers."

Together they helped Dwight out of the car and wheeled him through the lobby to their ground floor hotel room. Sabrina walked Norma back to her car. They hugged again and as Norma walked to the driver's door, Sabrina climbed into the passenger seat and closed the door.

"Ok Norma, we have never kept a single thing from each other over all these years, the good times and the heartbreaks. We've been the best of girlfriends since France. And we share a son who's getting married. Now tell me what's wrong. Dwight's right, you do look like hell."

"Too many Camels for too many years, Sabrina. I have inoperable lung cancer."

Sabrina took an involuntary breath and shuttered.

"Oh Jesus no...no, no Norma...oh my no...shit!" Sabrina cried.

"Afraid so."

"Does Timothy know?"

"No! Only Dr. Smith, and now you. No one is to know for now. Let's get the kids through their special day ok?"

"Are you in pain? Does it hurt you?"

"It hurts when I cough...a lot. And I'm so damned tired. All I want to do is take a nap. I'm more tired now than when I worked the night shift all those years."

"You have a productive cough?"

"A little bloody, especially in the mornings."

"Oh, I'm heartbroken for you Norma. I feel so bad."

The two ladies, who had been friends since they first met at a M.A.S.H. field hospital on the battlefields in France during World War II, who had shared secrets all the following years, who had watched their great men grow old and then endured the death of Charles, held hands and cried in the front seat of Norma's silver Mercedes Benz on the eve of their son's wedding.

"It's ok. Let's get Timothy married. Then I can join Charles. I miss him so much.

"Not a word Sabrina."

"Promise."

Then Norma drove home.

That evening Poor Joe's was rocking. "Let's do ours different," Carla had suggested to Timothy. "Let's have a celebration the night before the wedding and then we can just slip away after the ceremony."

"Let's," Timothy agreed.

Wendell had "commissioned" Doug and Ralph to build a little stage against the west wall of Poor Joe's for this occasion.

And there she stood on the new stage next to David Chown on the keyboards. Born in Aibonito, Puerto Rico, Miriam was a beauty to behold. Her dark brown hair cascaded over each shoulder, outlining her beautiful Caribbean face. Her sparkling brown eyes radiated excitement and her lips expressed a shy smile as she sang.

"Oh wow, where did Timothy find her? She's beautiful!" exclaimed Wayne.

"Carla found her, asked her to sing at their reception and wedding," Jonathon said proudly because he had an inside scoop. "Her and that guy on keyboards whose name is David are real big in Traverse City."

And then the assembled crowd at Poor Joe's heard a melodic voice like none they had ever heard. Miriam's voice started low with a little rasp and then, as the song progressed, achieved octaves never before heard by anyone present.

"Damn, she's really good. She's better than Carla!" exclaimed Jonathon.

"That's what Carla said," Wendell added.

The building trembled. Song after song, clapping and laughter and shouts of joy could be felt for blocks.

Timothy introduced Gary Jamison to Wendell. The two men grasped each other by the shoulders.

"Thank you man," Wendell finally said to Gary. "Don't remember the ride up the ladder on your back, but I sure do thank you for all you did that day."

"Hell man, I was using you as a shield cuz they were shooting at me…and I got a free ride to the Hancock."

"Well I thank you Gary. I thank you very much."

And with that, Gary Jamison pulled a bottle of Raynal rare old French brandy from his hip pocket and said, "Two glasses please."

Gary and Wendell spent the remainder of the party sitting at Jonathan's table, drinking brandy and becoming the best of friends.

Miriam Pico's voice and David Chown's Scottish smile, as his talented fingers tickled the keyboard, said it all. They were putting on the performance of their lives, driven by the enthusiasm and the love of the Big Bay crowd.

Stanley and Danielle held each other tight as they danced to Miriam singing, "You've Got a Friend" and then, "The Way You Look Tonight." Carla led Timothy by the hand to the dance floor and they snuggled close as they danced to "Cheek to Cheek" and "Someone to Watch Over Me."

Mariam was singing "So In Love" when Timothy and Carla danced over to where Stanly and Danielle were dancing.

"When are you guys going to tie the knot?" Carla asked as the couples gently bumped.

"You guys first. We'll see!" answered Danielle as Stanley smiled.

Poor Joe's closed at 10pm as instructed by Timothy.

Miriam was singing "At Last" as Timothy and Carla left the building.

"Big day tomorrow friends," he said with a huge smile and a wave of his right hand as he left the building with Carla.

As she drove out of the parking lot, Carla rolled down her window and shouted to Timothy, "Tomorrow I will be married to the man of my dreams!"

* * *

The Marine Corps Honor Guard stood at attention on either side of the sidewalk which led to the doors of the Big Bay Methodist Church. There was not an empty seat in the building.

Norma and Sabrina and Dwight sat side by side in the front row.

Timothy entered the church from a side door with the pastor and his Best Man, Stanley. When he saw Norma, Sabrina, and Dwight sitting together, he walked down off the podium and kissed each one on the forehead. He had tears in his eyes when he returned, and Stanley handed him a tissue.

Carla's bridesmaids were Jillena and Carmen. Her Maid of Honor was Danielle. The beauty of Danielle walking down the aisle astonished Stanley and made his hands sweat.

Everyone stood as "The Wedding March" began. The sight of his bride walking towards him made Timothy's knees a little weak. "Don't let me look silly up here Stanley," he whispered.

"You're going to do just fine soldier," Stanley whispered in reply.

And with the exchange of vows, Timothy Fife and Carla Fife became Mr. and Mrs. Timothy Fife. As the newlyweds walked down the aisle hand in hand, Miriam Pico sang "Tupelo Honey" from the choir balcony:

"She's as sweet as tupelo honey
She's an angel of the first degree
She's as sweet as tupelo honey
Just like honey from the bee."

Timothy smiled because he knew it was true.

Hand in hand they walked beneath the tunnel of swords extended over their heads by the Honor Guards. When they reached the end of the tunnel, the final Marine slapped Carla on the butt with his sword and then resumed attention.

"I should have warned you," Timothy laughed as they climbed in their car and headed for the airport.

"Where are they headed?" asked Doug.

"Mackinac Island," replied Stanley.

Chapter 25

Life is No Accident

"Oh my gosh, honey, I still have Heather living in my spare room," Carla exclaimed to Timothy as they boarded the ferry to Mackinac Island. "I've had so much on my mind I forgot all about Heather and Justice living with me."

"Yup, that would make things a bit awkward from time to time. I'll call Wendell tomorrow and have the boys move my stuff to your place. I mean our place. And Heather can live in my apartment. Doug will keep her safe."

Mackinac Island was ablaze with fall colors of red, various shades of yellows and bronze, all outlined by the blue waters of Lake Huron. As the ferry pulled up to the docks, Carla and Timothy stood at the bow, awestruck.

"I thought it was beautiful last summer; this is like heaven," Carla said softly as she rested her head on Timothy's left shoulder.

"This is heaven, honey. With you here, this is heaven."

Carla had reserved the same room at The Grand Hotel where Timothy had proposed to her. They unpacked the suitcases and took a brief nap. Then they took a horse drawn taxi to The Woods restaurant for their first meal together as husband and wife.

Carla had reserved the same table, up the steps and to the left, that they had used on their engagement night. To her delight, they had the same Jamaican waiter who recognized them immediately.

"You do look gorgeous this evening madam," the waiter proclaimed as he pulled out Carla's chair.

"I'm a married lady now, Isaiah! I'm very happy."

Turning to Timothy, the waiter continued, "And you sir are a very fortunate man indeed."

"Yes I am Isaiah; I am a most fortunate man." And Timothy sat down, staring at the love of his life.

Without taking his eyes from Carla's, Timothy continued, "I believe we will start with a bottle of Chalone Pinot Noir."

"Yes sir, lot number 111. The island is the only place in the world you will find that bottle; the owner of The Grand Hotel purchased that entire vintage you know."

"Didn't know that. It has special memories for us Isaiah."

"Well sir, I do believe we can secure a bottle for the two of you to take home as well, to commemorate your wedding!"

"You are a very sweet man," Carla said as she pulled this gentle Jamaican man with gray hair towards her. She kissed him on the cheek.

Timothy and Carla ordered the identical meals they had eaten on their engagement evening.

"I think we should make this a tradition," Timothy said as they finished eating, "every year on our anniversary."

"Yes, let's!"

The next day Timothy and Carla visited the historic Fort Mackinac which they hadn't toured during their summer vacation. Every morning they walked down the hill from The Grand Hotel and followed Cadotte Street until it intersected with Huron Street. Then they turned left and walked east past Horn's Bar and Marc's Double Oven Bakery where the sweet smell of the morning cinnamon rolls wafted through the open door. Every morning the lovers were greeted by the clip-clopping sound of the whooshing horse drawn street sweeper and a wave from the driver as they walked to the marina and JL Beanery's Coffee Shoppe. There they would sip dark Italian coffee at sunrise and make plans for the day. On Wednesday, they rented a carriage pulled by a horse named Jack and spent the entire day exploring the history-saturated island.

Every evening they would stop at The Mustang Lounge for a "night-cap," even though there was a new bartender.

"Where's the old bartender, Gary?" Timothy asked one night.

"He left for a wedding last week and no one has heard from him since," replied the new bartender.

"Oh. Anyone try to find him?"

"Why? You know him?" asked the new sandy haired bartender suspiciously.

"Old war buddy."

"The owner said he was kinda messed up from the war. Told me he talked to some guy named Wendell at a Poor Joe's bar who said he didn't know where Gary was, so I got this job full time."

"That war left all of us messed up young man. Lieutenant Gary Jamison is one of the bravest men I know."

"I suppose…what you drinking soldier…on the house."

"I've had plenty, thanks. Catch you next time."

Timothy and Carla walked slowly up the hill leading to The Grand. The street was softly illuminated by ancient street lamps.

"I'm very happy Timothy."

"Me too Carla. I've never been happier."

The night concierge hailed them as they entered the hotel lobby.

"I have a message for you Mr. Fife." And he handed Timothy a small envelope with The Grand Hotel seal on it.

Timothy opened it once they reached their room.

"What's it say?"

"Stanley wants me to call him….says it's not urgent."

"Think he's still up?"

"Let's find out."

Timothy dialed Stanley's home number.

"Hello."

"Hi Stanley. Hope I'm not interrupting anything."

"Timothy? What time is it?"

"0100."

"Ok. I'm awake now. You could have waited until morning buddy."

"Afraid I'd miss you. What's up?"

"Wendell has a situation at Poor Joe's and is completely befuddled. This gal shows up driving a big old black Bentley. Her name is Rose and she claims to own a chain of night clubs in Nevada and California. She told Wendell she wants to buy Poor Joe's. Wendell told her it wasn't for sale and that you were on your honeymoon. She just patted Wendell on the head and told him, "Every couple deserves a good honeymoon. I'll just wait.""

"Well Wendell's right, it's not for sale. Why didn't he call me?"

"He is totally intimidated by her and he didn't want to ruin your honeymoon. I told him I was going to check up on you guys anyway."

"So you *did* want to ruin my honeymoon, huh?" Timothy laughed.

"Wait until you meet this Rose. She has a demanding persona."

"She got you intimidated too?"

"No, I haven't been intimidated since that first night at the hospital when your mother looked me up and down and announced I could call her Chief. I was scared to death."

"Yup, Mother can put the fear of God in a person. Well, tell Wendell I'll deal with Rose when I get back next week, and not to give her any free drinks."

"Ok….you guys having fun?"

"Beyond my wildest dreams, Stan. I recommend marriage."

"Of course you do….she's sitting right next to you."

"Hi Stanley, this is Carla. Get married. Good night." And with a laugh, she hung up the phone.

"What was that all about, and what's not for sale?" Carla asked.

"Some gal by the name of Rose walked into Poor Joe's and wants to buy it. She supposedly owns several nightclubs out west, I have no idea how she found Poor Joe's. I'll deal with her when we get back."

Carla sat quietly on the side of the bed for a minute. Then she said, "I have something to show you." And she took a letter from her purse.

"This came last week. We had enough to do without discussing this." Carla handed the letter to Timothy.

Timothy slowly unfolded it while staring at his wife. Then he read, "Dear Carla Fife, Our talent and celebrity scouts have given me your name with their recommendation that you be considered for a recording contract with Imagine Recording Studios. I have personally listened to several demo recordings which you made while residing here in Nashville. I must say that I am very impressed with your voice and your talent. I am prepared to offer you a five year contract with Imagine Studios, including at least two records and weekly appearances at the Tin Roof Blues House. Please contact me at your earliest convince. Sincerely, Karl S. Remington, President, Imagine Studios."

"Wow ……..Carla….wow. Holy cow, this is really something, honey!"

"It's an opportunity Timothy, that's all. What's most important in our lives is you and me. Nothing trumps us. I've spent my life looking for you and I won't let anything blur our love, or separate us, not even this."

"Well……We could sell Poor Joe's and move to Nashville. I could be your manager!"

"I love the sound of that ……..my manager. Let me introduce you to my manager….and the man I sleep with!"

"We'll get all this sorted out when we get home. I'll deal with Rose and you call Mr. Remington and we'll see what happens."

"I don't think Rose showing up was an accident. I was wondering how to approach this offer, and just like that Rose shows up."

"Remarkable," Timothy replied.

The honeymooners spent a total of twelve days on Mackinac Island. As they became more familiar with each other, their love united the couple in a way they never thought possible. They become one.

Timothy and Carla Fife returned to Big Bay on a Thursday.

Carla stayed at their condo to sort through wedding gifts, and to contact Imagine Studios. Timothy drove over to Poor Joe's in Carla's car.

"Oh man, am I ever glad to see you!" Wendell exclaimed as Timothy walked through the back door of Poor Joe's. And Wendell pointed towards Jonathon's table against the southwest wall.

Not easily missed, Rose had an aura about her, a persona that demanded attention and respect. There she sat at Jonathon's table, laughing and telling bawdy jokes and buying the boys drinks.

She stood up when she saw Timothy. Without hesitation, she strode over and introduced herself.

"Hello Timothy. I'm Rose Jackson. I hope you and your bride had a fantastic honeymoon."

"It's nice to meet you Rose Jackson. Thank you, we had a wonderful time on Mackinac Island."

"Never been there."

"You should try it next summer; it is a trip back in time."

"Someplace we can talk, Timothy?"

"Use my room," Doug said from a bar stool.

Timothy and Rose walked up the stairs and entered Doug's room at the top of the landing. There was a 12 gauge pump shotgun lying on his bed.

"Is it loaded?" Rose asked in surprise.

"Yup. Doug is a good guy and someone you want on your side."

"Good to know."

"I hear you have some Italian friends in St. Paul as well, Timothy."

"I used to work there…that's all. You don't miss a lick do you?"

"Try not ….I try not. You going to sell Poor Joe's to me?"

"First things first, Rose. You've gotten to know the men who live here. They're my friends. They would do absolutely anything for me, and I for them. If I sell the place it will be part of the contract that they're not to be displaced....ever."

"Oh I wouldn't change a thing Timothy; I like Poor Joe's just the way it is. Kind of quaint, like nothing I've ever owned. They can all stay."

"And I want Wendell to stay on as the manager," Timothy added.

"Sounds good to me. I have no intention of running the place. I might take the piano player with me though. I like him."

"Jonathon?"

"He's quite a guy."

"That he is, that he is."

"How much, Timothy?"

"Make an offer, and I'll talk it over with my wife tonight."

"I was thinking three hundred and fifty thousand."

"That's a fair offer. Carla and I will discuss it.

"Bye the way, how did you know that Poor Joe's even existed?"

"An old friend of yours by the name of Vincent mentioned it to me a few months back."

"Oh Vincent...I saved his kid from burning up in his wrecked Corvette a few years ago, when I was working in St Paul."

"I've had several transactions with Vincent in Vegas over the years." Rose continued, "He's an honorable man."

"That he is Rose; a man of his word."

Rose walked down the stairs in front of Timothy, who gave a thumbs up signal to the assembled inhabitants below.

Timothy had a mixed excitement in his head as he drove home to Carla. He loved Poor Joe's. He adored Carla. Yet, his heart was heavy with the thoughts of loss and the separation from the men who he knew would give their lives for him without question.

"Hi honey. How did your conversation go with Imagine Studios?"

"You are *not* going to believe what they offered me Timothy!"

"Try me."

"A one million dollar contract to record 3 albums, and to sing at the Tin Roof Blues House 40 Saturdays a year for the next five years, plus royalties from the record sales!"

"Oh my God, Carla! What did you tell him?"

"I said I had to talk it over with my husband and that I would call him back tomorrow."

"What did he say?"

"He said he respected that. He told me that was the first time anyone had ever given him that answer."

"Wow, one million dollars. Are you happy?"

"Thrilled, but I'm not going anyplace unless you can go with me. What happened at Poor Joe's?"

Timothy related the conversations with Rose, and the proposed deal which allowed the current upstairs inhabitants to remain.

"She offered me three hundred and fifty thousand. I paid eighty-nine thousand twenty years ago."

"Are you happy, Timothy?"

"I am; I'm very happy for us. I'll tell Rose we have a deal in the morning."

"I'll call Mr. Remington in the morning and accept the contract."

"You know you're going to miss Doug and Wayne and Wendell, and Jonathon. And the morning National Anthem on Ralph's trumpet."

"Sure will, at least for a while. They'll make for good memories and a few laughs when we live in Nashville."

"We're going to start a brand new life together. This is just thrilling!" Carla exclaimed as she snuggled as close as she could to the man she loved. "And I will help you with the heartache, I promise."

"I know you will."

* * *

The ringing phone awaked Timothy and Carla the next morning at four thirty.

"Timothy this is Stanley. I have Norma in the ER; Sabrina and Dwight are with her."

"What's wrong Stan, what happened? Sabrina and Dwight are still here?"

"Your mother is coughing up blood. You and Carla need to come down here."

Dr. Smith met them as they entered the Emergency Room.

"Hi Lavern, what's wrong with Mom?"

"This is breaking my heart Timothy. Norma has inoperable lung cancer."

"Oh shit......oh nuts...damn it...damn! How long has she known Doc?"

"About six months. I'm so sorry. She didn't want you and Carla to know for as long as possible. She didn't want to ruin the wedding."

"Well... that would be like her. What room is she in?"

"Room Four; follow me."

Norma was sitting up with the head of the ER stretcher at forty-five degrees. She held a Yanker Suction in her right hand and suctioned herself after each cough. The suction tubing leading to the wall canister showed a frothy bright red blood.

"Just get away and let me do it myself. I suctioned people before your daddy reached puberty," Norma scolded the new ER nurse.

"Hello Mother. You look like hell," Timothy said as they entered the room.

"Is that any way to speak to your mother? How was the honeymoon Carla?"

"It was wonderful Norma. I'm so sorry...."

"Oh hell, this is what I get for smoking all those damn Camels all those years. Remember those nights Stanley....nurses' station was blue with smoke......stupid."

"I didn't have to buy a single cigarette," Stanley admitted.

Sabrina was standing next to the stretcher holding Norma's left hand. Carla walked around the stretcher and took the Yanker Suction away from Norma and handed it to Danielle who had just entered the room. Timothy moved next to Dwight and put his right hand on Dwight's shoulder.

"Stanley, I want you to call that Jillena who runs the Hospice Unit and get me a bed. I'm not long for this world and I'll be damned if I'm going out a burden to my family," Norma proclaimed.

"Yes Chief."

"Good to see I taught you the proper respect."

Everyone in the room snickered softly.

Chapter 26

One Tough Lady

The two friends sat in Stanley's office located just down the hall from the Cardiac Care Unit, with the door closed.

"Saw your mom this morning Timothy. She is one tough lady. I've never known anyone like her. She sure was a big help to me when I first got into nursing."

"She's something else. Once she makes up her mind about the right way to do a thing, she's a rock."

"I asked her how she was doing, and she looked at me with those piercing blue eyes and said, 'Dying isn't hard Stanley. I've seen hundreds of people die and so have you. It's the living that's hard. I wish I could go back and do it all over again. I did the best I could, I think. Now I can't wait to be with Charles again. I love that man very much. Stanley, I want you to remember this; love is the only thing that matters……the only thing young man. Cherish love…,' and then she closed her eyes."

"That's something coming from Norma. Wow, she's a marshmallow under that shell, huh?"

"I guess we saw what she wanted us to see, Timothy."

"How much longer do you think she has?"

"I just don't know. She's one tough lady. I think when she decides it's time, she'll be gone. I just don't know. Why?"

"Carla and I have some big changes looming in our lives. I can't bring myself to sell Poor Joe's while Mom's still alive."

"What? You're selling Poor Joe's? You're going to sell to that Rose lady?"

"Yeah I am, but I can't bring myself to do it while Mom is still with us. She loves that old bar."

"I think she would say just sell the damn place and get on with your life. I can hear her say it, can't you?"

"Yup, but I still can't do it. I told Rose yesterday morning that we'd finalize the sale when the time was right and we shook hands and she left in her black Bentley with Jonathon in the passenger seat next to her."

"What! She took Jonathon with her?"

"Said she needed a piano player in Reno and that she kinda liked him ….a lot."

"Well good for Jonathon I guess."

"And that's not all that's going on. Carla has a recording contract with Imagine Recording Studios in Nashville. We're going to move to Nashville at some point."

"That's wonderful news. I'm very happy for you guys. Carla must be thrilled!"

"We're pretty excited. That's the only reason I agreed to sell the bar."

"Danielle is going to be thrilled for you guys too."

"They're having lunch together today, Stan. She's going to know all about it."

"Well, she's probably telling Carla all about my job offer too."

"What?"

"Remember the nurse Darlene who moved up from Marathon and then died from ovarian cancer?"

"Sure do."

"Well come to find out, Darlene and the Director of Nursing at Fisherman's Hospital in Marathon were close friends and they talked on the phone a lot after Darlene moved north. I just received a phone call from the Director last night. She said Darlene raved about me and told this lady that I was the best RN and manager she had ever known. She told the Director that if she ever had a chance, she should steal me away. It was an embarrassing thing to listen to."

"And she called you with an offer?"

"Yup, said the hospital's Cardiac Care Manager had retired and she had been saving my number for just this occasion."

"What are you going to do?"

"Danielle and I talked it over last night. We both have a month of vacation saved. I think we're going to fly to Miami and take a little vacation in the Keys, stop in Marathon and talk to the Director, and then drive down to Key West."

"Holy mackerel!"

"Life goes on Timothy; changes come and people leave, but life goes on. We just need to always remember what your mother told me this morning because it's the truth no matter where we go or what we do."

"Love is all that matters."

"That's it my friend. Now you and Carla go tell your mother the good news and your plans. She'll be thrilled for you."

"We'll tell her tonight."

Chapter 27

Low Sodium Chicken Gravy

"Code Gray......CCU," the hospital operator blurted out on the public address system. Then the message arrived on Stanley's pager.

He bolted from his office and turned left towards the CCU just as Doctor McCaferty backed out of Room Five, under a barrage of obscenities.

"You come in here again and I will rip off your head and shit down your neck!" screamed a crazed voice.

And then a fully loaded lunch tray flew out the door and covered the retreating Cardiologist with broiled chicken breast, mashed potatoes with low sodium gravy, green beans and blueberry cobbler.

"What the hell Jack?" Stanley asked as the two met outside the raving patient's door.

"I don't think he likes me."

"Really."

"I was just explaining the pros and cons for a cardiac cath. and he took offense to the offer."

"Go finish lunch Jack," Stanley suggested with a smile as he swiped some blueberry cobbler from Dr. McCaferty's white lab coat and tasted it. "Yum."

And then Stanley turned 180 degrees and walked directly towards the shouting man.

"Mister, you sit down and shut up," Stanley commanded, "or I will let those guys come in here and hogtie you to the bed."

The man stopped mid-scream and stared at Stanley who had a look gained by one hundred bouts in the boxing ring.

"I mean it; your choice pilgrim."

The man looked over Stanley's shoulder at the two orderlies and an orthopedic tech staring at him.

He sat down on the bed.

"What are you trying to do, kill yourself man? You've had a heart attack and now look at you carrying on like this is a bar fight. I'm surprised we're not doing CPR on you right now."

The man sat on the edge of his bed saying nothing, watching the blood dripping on the floor from his right forearm where he had ripped the IV catheter out during his tirade.

"Mind if I sit down?" Stanley asked, as he motioned the anxious staff away from the door.

"Nope."

Stanley sat on the bloody linen, next to the patient.

"You know, you look a lot like Jimmy Hoffa--same haircut, same build. You two could have been brothers."

The man stared at Stanley for several minutes before he spoke.

"You knew Jimmy did you?"

"He used to have a summer cabin up the river several miles. I would see him from time to time before he disappeared. I knew his son better."

"I was one of Jimmy Hoffa's body guards. I worked for him," the man quietly growled.

"What was it like working for Jimmy Hoffa? There must have been some tense moments."

"Let's put it this way; what's your name?"

"Stanley."

"Let's put it this way, Stanley. If you're not the toughest dog in the junk yard, you don't get off the porch."

"You accustomed to being in charge, huh?"

"You got to be Stanley."

"And now you're not in charge of anything, and to top it all off, you're scared to death."

The man stared at Stanley with disbelief.

"Wouldn't you be?"

"Don't know. I'm not the one with the broken heart sitting here dripping blood all over the floor. But here's what I think; not knowing doesn't make anything better. If I were in your place I'd say let's go take a look and fix what needs to be fixed. Kinda like taking a sputtering car to your mechanic. He's useless if you don't let him lift the hood and take a look."

The man looked at Stanley and tears trickled out of both eyes.

"You got me there Stanley. Can you stop this bleeding and tell that Doctor I'm sorry and we can do his test."

"I'll tell him. He's a good guy even though he has friends in the Irish Mafia."

"Really?"

"No…just kidding."

"Will you go with me down for that test?"

"Yes I will."

Stanley walked back to the nurses' station where Dr. McCaferty was sitting, wearing a clean new lab coat.

"Finished lunch, huh, Jack?"

"You're a funny man."

"He says he's sorry and has signed the permits and would like you to do his cath."

"Seriously?"

"He used to work for Jimmy Hoffa…was one of his body guards. He's just scared cuz things are swirling out of his control. And I told him you had friends in the Irish Mafia."

"You're kidding."

"Yup. I'm kidding Jack."

* * *

After work, Stanley drove up the hill to Danielle's condo.

Danielle poured him a glass of Basil Hayden's on the rocks as he walked through the door. She held a Collins glass filled with club soda and a wedge of lime.

"How was your day? I heard a Code Gray called in CCU."

Stanley recalled the afternoon events in detail.

"Sometimes I think you take too much risk, honey."

"Naw….what's the worst that can happen? I've been knocked out before, doesn't hurt a bit."

"You idiot."

"Didn't cause any drain bamage either."

"Exactly my point."

"Oh, Timothy stopped in my office this morning. We talked about Norma for a while and I told him I thought he should tell his mom all about their plans, that she would be thrilled for them."

"I had lunch with Carla today in the cafeteria. She thought I should tell you something too."

"What's that?"

"Remember when I thought I had the GI flu a couple of weeks ago?"

"The night we canceled dinner out at Benjamin's Seafood?"

"Yes."

"It wasn't the stomach flu."

"What then?"

"We're going to have a baby."

"Holy mackerel……..you and me……you and me… mom and dad! You ok with this?"

"I can't think of another man who I'd rather have as the father of my child, Stanley. I adore you."

"I love you Danielle. You want to get married?

"Is that a proposal?"

"Yes….do you want to get married?"

"I accept your proposal Mr. McMillen. I will be honored to be Mrs. Danielle McMillen. Let's go on our vacation first. Let's go to the Keys and make our plans."

"Wow, this has been quite a day. Just wait until Ramona hears how I've ruined your honor."

"Oh shut up!"

Chapter 28

Taps for Norma

Stanley was sleeping soundly, lying on his left side, when the telephone began to ring. It rang and rang. In his mind the ringing seemed to be part of a dream. Finally, he slowly opened his right eye and looked at the dimly lit GE clock radio that he had kept since college. The hands on the clock pointed to 2:33. He groped for the telephone on the nightstand, knocking his watch, glasses and a glass of water to the floor.

"Damnit!

"Hello."

"Stanley…..this is Timothy…….Mom just died."

The news felt cold, like frost settling over his bare body, as the words struck his mind. Stanley shuttered.

"I'll be right there."

"This is harder than I ever imagined. I need you. Carla is holding Mom's hand and has her head buried on Mom's chest and is just sobbing."

"I'll pick up Danielle and be right there my friend….on my way."

"Sabrina and Dwight are here. I think they're in some sort of shock, just staring at her, Stanley. This is awful."

Stanley drove up to Danielle's condo and together they headed for Big Bay General. A few blocks from the hospital a patrol car tried to pull them over for speeding. Stanley refused to stop until they arrived in the ER parking lot.

"You were doing seventy in a twenty-five Stanley," the young officer announced as Stanley opened the driver's door.

"Timothy's mother just died and he needs us."

"Oh…sorry." He walked back to his patrol car and drove away into the dark night.

It was as Timothy had described on the telephone. Norma lay in repose on the bed. Carla was sitting in a chair on the right side of the bed, holding Norma's hand, her face was buried in the blankets, sobbing and talking to Norma softly.

Sabrina stood on the other side of the bed, holding Norma's left hand and staring in a sort of disbelief. Dwight sat in his wheelchair and was holding Sabrina's hand. The old soldier was crying.

"I am so glad you came," Timothy said as they entered the room. The two best friends embraced and Timothy's body began to convulse in sobs.

Danielle kneeled down on both knees beside Carla and wrapped her arms around her friend.

"You know that Norma and Charles are together watching us right now," Danielle whispered.

"I know. I know, and I can hear her telling us to knock it off and get on with our lives. I sure am going to miss this crusty old bitch. I love you Norma."

Sabrina cleared her throat, "They're together now, the way they always dreamed. I'm going to give the funeral. Timothy, you call that pastor at the Methodist church …or you Stanley, I don't care, and tell that man that I will be speaking at Norma's funeral."

They all stayed together in Norma's room and slowly accommodated their minds to this loss in their lives which was not repairable.

"I'll call Pastor Long this morning and make the arrangements," Timothy said as they walked out of the hospital.

"I want to sing her favorite song, 'What a Friend,'" Carla said as they walked to the parking lot. "I'm going to sing, 'What a Friend,' Timothy," she repeated.

"Mom will like that."

The day progressed and the grief came in waves.

For Stanley it was the loss of a mentor. "She was one tough lady who taught me more than I ever learned in college," he commented to Danielle. "Chief told me the very first night I worked with her, 'You sure look young, but don't worry, we'll teach you more than you learned in college.' I can hear her say it now. Damn, she was something."

For Timothy it was the loss of the mother he had longed for as a child and finally found after all those years during a conversation in Poor Joe's.

For Sabrina it was the loss of her only true friend.

This group of friends worked together making arrangements for Norma Bouvier, retired battle-hardened Army Major, retired Registered Nurse extraordinaire, mother and ardent friend. To each it seemed as if they were caught in a Shakespearian tragedy, not quite real.

Dwight called the President of the Citadel, requesting an Honor Guard of Cadets. They arrived on a military green bus.

Timothy contacted Jonathon in Reno, and purchased airline tickets for him. "Norma would love for you to play the piano."

"I'll be there Timothy."

Carla called Miriam Pico.

"Miriam, I want to sing 'What a Friend' at Norma's funeral. I'm not sure I can get through it without breaking down. If I pay for your ticket, will you fly here and sing it with me?"

"You don't have to pay for my ticket, Carla. I remember Norma very well. I'll be by your side and we'll sing it like it's never been sung before."

Ralph practiced playing taps on his trumpet.

The church that not that long ago was packed for a glorious wedding was now again packed with the same people for a funeral.

"This is my best friend who we're saying goodbye to here today," Sabrina started. She was standing tall in the pulpit and she had a glow about her head.

"I have known this lady since the battlefields of France. We have been side by side throughout this life, even when separated by miles and circumstances. I have never known a truer human being or a kinder soul. Her first concern was never for herself, and she never wanted attention or credit. This lady we lay in the ground today beside her beloved Charles is a true example of love that has walked among us. We are all better people for having known her."

And with that, Sabrina turned and looked up to the choir loft where Carla and Miriam stood side by side with their arms around each other.

Jonathon began playing the piano....

> "What a friend we have in Jesus,
> All our sins and griefs to bear!
> What a privilege to carry
> Everything to Him in prayer.
> O what peace we often forfeit,
> O what needless pain we bear.
> All because we do not carry
> Everything to God in Prayer.
> Have we trials and temptations?
> Is there trouble anywhere?
> We should never be discouraged;
> Take it to the Lord in prayer.
> Can we find a friend so faithful
> Who will all our sorrows share?
> Jesus knows our every weakness;
> Take it to the Lord in prayer

> Are we weak and heavy laden
> Cumbered with a load of care.
> Precious Savior, still our refuge;
> Do thy friends despise, forsake thee
> Take it to the Lord in prayer.
> In his arms he'll take you and shield thee;
> thou will find solace there."

All those present that afternoon claim that the sound from the loft was a choir of angels.

Norma Bouvier, RN (Chief) was buried next to Chief of Police Charles Johnson, high on the bluffs overlooking Big Bay as Ralph played taps.

Chapter 29

The Shower Squadron

S tanley always took the stairs up to his office. "I'll take the
elevator when the stairs are broke," was his standard reply
when urged to take the elevators with coworkers. He had just about reached
his office door when a voice arrived from behind him.

"I hear you're going to be a daddy." It was Ramona, the Director of
Nursing.

Stanley turned around to face the anticipated inquisition.

"That news sure is spreading fast. I just learned myself last week,
Ramona."

"All the nurses are excited for Danielle. Nancy, Carla, Carmen and
Jillena are planning a baby shower. Now don't you mess this up, Stanley.
You going to marry this wonderful lady?"

"That's what I love about you Ramona......right to the point. Well
for your information, Danielle has accepted my proposal; told me she will
love to be Mrs. Danielle McMillen."

"Well good. You are both exceptional in my book and I wish you much happiness together."

"Thank you! Is it ok now if we live together?" Stanley inquired with a grin.

"Hell no, it's not ok. She's an honorable lady. Not so sure about you," the Director replied. Then she winked at him.

"That's why I don't wear a nursing cap, boss."

"Just get to work Stanley." And she walked down the hall towards the Cardiac Care Unit.

"Hey, Ramona. I need to talk to you sometime soon."

She turned around and walked back towards Stanley.

"How's now? Now is good for me."

"Now will work for me too." And they walked into Stanley's office. Ramona closed the door before she sat down in the wooden chair next to the desk.

"Darlene's old Director of Nursing at Fisherman's Hospital in Marathon called me. She offered me the position of CCU Manager."

"She doesn't even know you."

"Well apparently Darlene told her all about me and told her to steal me the first chance she got. The current manager is retiring, so she called me."

"Well.......?"

"Danielle and I are taking a vacation in the Keys next month. We thought we'd stop at Fisherman's on our way down to Key West and at least talk to her."

"That's what I would do. No harm in talking Stanley. Just give me fair warning if it's more than talk."

"I promise."

Ramona got up and opened the door. As she was leaving, she poked her head back in. "I sure will miss you Stanley." She didn't go to CCU, but rather took the elevator to the ground floor and her office. She closed the door.

Danielle was working the afternoon shift, covering for staff vacations, and Stanley was bored. After watching the evening news, he walked the seven blocks from Grant Street to Poor Joe's. When he entered, the residents were all huddled around what had been known as Jonathon's table.

"We need a consultation, Stanley," Morris said.

"Yeah, a consultation!" chimed in Ralph.

"On any particular subject?" Stanley shot back.

"The baby shower," Wayne replied. "We ain't never been part of no baby shower."

"What are you guys talking about?"

"The baby shower for Danielle; the nurses are giving your honey a baby shower," Wendell chimed in.

"And you guys are invited?"

"Nope......gonna be a surprise," Pete answered with a big smile.

"That it will be guys," Stanley replied as he turned and looked at Timothy who was standing behind the counter shaking his head.

"This means a lot to the guys."

"Yeah Stanley....means a lot to us," Doug said. "You guys mean a lot to us fellows."

"Ok, we'll talk about it."

"You can't say anything to the ladies," Wayne added.

"Oh trust me, I won't say a word."

For the next three hours these men made plans to contribute to the nurses' baby shower. The more they drank, the more excited they became. Stanley left at eleven thirty and walked home. It actually amazed him, the love these men had for Danielle and himself. And he knew that no force on this earth would keep these men from showing up for this special occasion.

The nurses had several "secret" meetings to plan the shower while keeping Danielle "in the dark." Carmen, Jillena, Nancy and Ramona would meet in Jillena's condo to organize the event. Carmen was in charge of refreshments, Jillena in charge of the catering, Nancy in charge of decorations and Ramona took charge of secretly notifying the nursing staff.

"We need to do this in November. I know they're going to be in the

Keys for most of December," Ramona commented. Both Carmen and Jillena thought Ramona seemed sad when she mentioned this.

"Here, I brought the schedules. Look, November 18ᵗʰ everyone here is off, even Danielle," declared Ramona. "Let's plan on November 18ᵗʰ."

"Where should we have it?" asked Carmen

"Danielle has the perfect deck, and it's huge. The view is beautiful up there at night when the city is lit up down below. She has heaters so it won't matter if it's a little chilly. It's the perfect place for a party," Jillena stated.

"I'll bet we can get Stanley to take her out to dinner that evening and we'll have a grand surprise when she gets home!" exclaimed Nancy.

"Ok, we have a plan. I'll talk to Stanley," Ramona said.

The planning committee left Jillena's place with joy in their hearts for the surprise they were about to spring on their best friend.

"I'll call Sabrina," said Jillena as they walked to their cars. "She'll want to be here for this."

Timothy had left Poor Joe's early to spend time with Carla. They were sitting on the porch, cuddled up on the loveseat, listening to a Van Morrison album.

"I sure am glad we told Mom about our news and plans," Timothy said

"She seemed so happy for us. She just kept saying how proud of us she was, and how happy we made her....and then she just went to sleep....she just went to sleep."

"I think she just slipped over and gave Charles the news."

"I'm so happy I got a chance to meet her."

"She was something. I'm glad I got to meet her too!"

Just then the phone rang. Carla went inside and answered it.

"It's Stanley for you..."

"What's up?" Timothy spoke into the receiver.

"November 18th," Stanley replied, "just got the word from Ramona. I'm supposed to take Danielle out for a date and bring her back to a surprise party."

"We've got to have a meeting."

"Tomorrow at eight....Poor Joe's," Stanley replied.

"See you then."

"What was that about?" Carla asked.

Long pause...... "Ok honey, this has got to remain a secret. The boys down at the bar are planning on crashing Danielle's baby shower and joining the festivities."

"You have *got* to be kidding me...really?"

"I couldn't be more serious. Secret now...these guys love Stan and Danielle and there is no stopping them."

"Oh my God, this is going to be a party to remember, the nurses from the hospital throwing a baby shower, crashed by a squadron of drunks from Poor Joe's."

At 8pm that evening, the men assembled at Poor Joe's and stared at each other.

"Well what are we gonna do?" asked Pete.

"Never been to a baby shower; don't know," replied Doug.

"We ain't no good at buying baby stuff either," added Wendell.

The litany of the things they couldn't do and items which they were not qualified to purchase went on for the better part of an hour.

Suddenly Ralph jumped up from the table, spilling his glass of beer and exclaimed, "Hell men, we're wasting time saying things we're no good at. Let's do something we *are* good at.....let's bring the band and have a party!"

"What band?" was the question in unison.

"We take up a collection and fly Miriam and David back here. We get Jonathon back here and we have dueling pianos, and with Miriam on the guitar and me on the trumpet and Carla and Miriam singing, we have a band."

"How many beers did it take for you to come up with that?" Stanley asked in astonishment.

"Didn't count."

"I think it's a splendid idea," Timothy said. "In fact, Rose has to come back and finalize the purchase in November; I'll ask her to bring Jonathon along and aim for the 18th."

"I'll call Miriam and David," Stanley said.

"Oh boy, this is going to be great. Did I come up with a great one or what guys?" Ralph exclaimed.

"The best yet," Doug replied with a grin on his face. "This is going to be the best party ever."

The morning of November the 18th arrived. It was a crisp, cool morning with a forecast of sunshine and a high near 70.

"Beautiful day, honey, let's go out tonight ….a little date night," Stanley said on the phone from his office.

"I could cook us something special here Stan. I've been kinda tired lately."

"All the more reason to go out. Let's go to Benjamin's Seafood, last attempt was cancelled by the stomach flu remember?"

"You're a funny man. Ok, but let's go early. I need my beauty rest these days."

"I'll make a six thirty reservation."

"It's a date. Have a good day at work."

Stanley then called Ramona.

"I'm picking her up at six thirty. The place is yours."

He then called Timothy.

"Ok, the ladies will be arriving at six thirty. We probably should arrive at eight. Are Miriam and David here yet?"

"They're here and Rose just arrived half an hour ago with Jonathon."

"This is going to be something, Timothy. I hope I'm not in trouble when it's all over."

"I'll vouch for you."

"Yeah that'll help. See you tonight."

"Have a great date."

Stanley left work early and went home. After making a few phone calls, he drove from Grant Street up the hill to Danielle's condo.

"You look beautiful this evening, sweetheart," he said as she greeted him at the door.

"I don't have the flu tonight!" she replied with a radiant smile.

"Let's go eat." And they drove the rest of the way up the hill to Benjamin's Seafood Restaurant and the bluffs overlooking Big Bay.

Stanley could not remember the last time Danielle looked this beautiful, unless it was at Carla's wedding.

It was a mild evening and they sat on the deck under the heaters and looked down at the city.

"I love living here," Danielle said, as they held hands across the table.

"Well, I sure am happy you picked Big Bay. I love you very much. Your being here is like a miracle in my life. I have never been this happy."

"Remember the first time we touched?" Danielle asked.

"When we lifted that old man off the stretcher in the ER together."

"You do remember! That's the moment I knew why I'd come to Big Bay. Until then it was just an adventure and an excuse to get away from New Orleans and my crazy Cajun relatives...but at that moment I knew."

Mostly they talked, while just nibbling at the black grouper and scallops. Danielle apologized to the waiter when he inquired as to any problems with the food.

"It is delicious," she said. "We're not very hungry tonight, but this is a lovely evening."

As they walked down the wooden stairway that lead to the parking lot, Danielle squeezed Stanley's left arm and said, "This has been a perfect evening together. Thanks for insisting we go out."

Stanley maneuvered down the winding road. The sky was back-lit from the sunset and the frozen clouds above glistened a soft red.

"I think we should move in together. It would make going home less complicated," Stanley chuckled.

"Let's...when we get back from vacation. Which place should we sell?" Danielle asked.

"You're right, let's figure all that out while we're in the Keys. Who knows; might be selling both places!"

When they came around the last curve leading to her condo, there were at least twenty cars lining the street.

"What? Oh my, I hope everyone is ok. What do you think's going on Stanley?"

"Let's go check!"

They walked through Danielle's front door to an empty condo.

Then the French doors to the deck opened wide and a giant cheer went up as thirty-five nurses clapped for their dear comrade.

Sabrina hugged her and led Danielle out on the deck which was decorated for a baby shower. Danielle stood in the middle of her friends and cried with delight.

Stanley retreated to the street below and drove down the hill to Union Street.

"How'd it go?" Ralph asked excitedly as he walked into Poor Joe's.

"We had a great evening at Benjamin's and now she's with the ladies on her deck. The place is crowded. She is *so* excited!"

"I got the place wired for the sound system this morning," Timothy stated. "We should be all set for Miriam and David's equipment."

"How'd you pull that off? Danielle was home all day."

"Used to be in Special Forces, comes in handy some days. I worked from under the deck."

"Some days you scare me Timothy. Hell man, you'd die if you fell from there."

"I kept an eye on him, no worries," Doug said.

"You have no idea how much comfort that gives me Doug."

"Ok gang…..let's crash this party."

And the caravan, led by Timothy's 1956 Buick, drove up the hill to the baby shower. The car still had no muffler.

Miriam, a true sport, had agreed to lead the party of entertainers into the condo.

Danielle was sitting on the deck under a gas patio heater, surrounded by shower gifts and discarded wrapping paper, when the band walked through the condo and out onto the crowded deck. Everyone turned and looked up in surprise as Miriam announced, "Your entertainment for the evening has arrived. Meet the band."

David Chown walked out carrying an electronic keyboard. He was followed by Jonathon who was also carrying an electronic keyboard, and then Ralph with his trumpet and then Stanley who was carrying Miriam's guitar. Timothy whispered to Carla, who got up from her chair and joined them.

Then all the boys from Poor Joe's traipsed in shyly, and headed for the smorgasbord.

The joy and love expressed and shared that evening on Danielle's deck, high over Big Bay, filled the souls of the participants with a euphoria some had never experienced. The sorrow so magnificently expressed at Norma's funeral just weeks earlier was erased by the glorious celebration of this new life soon to be introduced to the world.

"I will talk to you later about this," Danielle giggled into Stanley's ear. "You are in so much trouble."

Chapter 30

A Note from Norma

"Carla and I told Mom all about our plans before she died." Timothy and Stanley sat side by side at the bar drinking black coffee, looking straight ahead at their reflections in the Goebel Beer mirror with gold lettering. The hands on the Winston clock above the mirror pointed to 8:37.

"I'm grateful you insisted we tell her. She was so happy with the news Stanley. It was like a great weight was lifted from her soul. We told her and she smiled and told us that she loved us very much and said, 'I'm very happy.' Then she just went to sleep. Thank you my friend."

"You're welcome."

"Rose and I finalize the sale tomorrow."

"I love this place. I'll never forget the night I was in here with the pool players consortium and announced that I was switching from Electrical Engineering to nursing. I thought the guys were going to die laughing."

"That's a few years before I moved from St. Paul and bought it.

The story is legend; everyone thought you were going to knock that newcomer out when he challenged your manhood."

"Yeah, that was kinda funny. I couldn't have, he had a pocket protector," Stanley said with a big grin.

"Not like the night Danielle's old boyfriend showed up from Alaska looking for you."

Stanley laughed. "Nope, not like that night!"

"I swear, both Doug and I tried to talk him out of it, but he was determined to settle some sort of score. So Doug and Ralph moved all the tables and chairs against the wall and I called you."

"Yeah, I thought *what the hell* and showed up to introduce myself. He had traveled all the way from Alaska after all."

"You walked in without your glasses on and all of us knew right then we had ringside seats."

"Well, I tried to be polite, introduced myself and he said his name was Steve Chase, right before he hit me."

"Yeah…on the arm. I have never seen a man move that quickly Stan. I mean it; your arm flew up and blocked that right punch! Your feet seemed to be gliding as you danced away…and then with a left-right-left, you knocked him out. Just like that."

"I don't remember the particulars. I felt kinda sorry for him."

"The boys were impressed. Jonathon especially was grateful that he hadn't come after you that night when you walked in and said you hated war."

Stanley laughed again. "He would have brought his bat."

"Did you ever tell Danielle?"

"Nope. And she never said anything about him contacting her."

"We have some great memories here," Timothy continued, "Like the night of Mom's retirement party when those bikers tried to crash it."

"Hell's Spawn, they called themselves. What a bunch of idiots," Stanley said with a reflective smile. "Charles and Doug sure did come through that night. I still think of that night every time I step over those buckshot holes in the floor."

"I think of the day Charles and I varnished the floor when I see those holes. Charles sat next to those holes and filled each one so they wouldn't collect dirt. He wanted to tell me that he was my father; he just couldn't for some reason.

"And," Timothy took a deep breath, "I didn't have the guts to ask him."

"Your party the night before the wedding--that was the best Timothy."

"Yes it was.

"I'm going to miss the guys who live here Stanley. I'll sure miss Doug, Morris, Jonathon and Wendell, Pete and Ralph and Wayne; they've experienced some absolute horror in their lives and not a one of them will ever whine about it. And believe it or not, I'm going to miss Dora's cooking. I knew this would be hard when Jonathon left with Rose; felt like one of the kids leaving home I guess."

"The guys love you. They know you understand....you've been there too."

"It's life Stan.

"It really hasn't been the same though," Timothy continued, "since I lost Jimmy last year. I loved that old dog. He was my best friend since Vietnam. He would ride around with me in St Paul, and never left my side since he was a pup...God I miss him."

"You could see it in his eyes. You would be out working the bar and he followed you with his big brown eyes. And those times when he felt you were being threatened, suddenly he was by your side glaring at the offender with his ears up and a 'you gotta be kidding' look on his face, and the problem melted away. Jimmy loved you without question."

"Just like the guys here Timothy, loyal without question. Each one, for very personal reasons, needs the comfort of this old building and each other. They are amazing human beings," Stanley said with admiration in his voice. "They made their choices and don't judge others for theirs."

"You have no idea how close those guys came to helping Dr. Nazar disappear when he was on your case. It's good he left town when he did, him and his brothers."

"He sure did think he was special. I owe you for helping on that one, Timothy."

"Naw."

"When are you guys moving to Nashville?"

"Carla's contract starts January first. We'll probably move the second week of December so we can be all settled in for our first Christmas together."

Stanley sighed.

"Danielle and I are going to be on vacation down in the Keys this December."

"We'll stay in touch Stanley. I'll give you a call when we get settled, with our new phone number and address. Nashville will be a great place to visit in the winter."

"Sure will."

And with that, the two men who had been at each other's side for all these years in Big Bay, turned on their bar stools and faced one another.

"I'm glad we're alone in here," Stanley said as he wiped at the tears with a bar napkin.

"No kidding. Special Forces don't shed tears."

"See you later buddy." And with a slap on Timothy's back, Stanley stepped over the buckshot holes in the hardwood floor and walked out the front door of Poor Joe's.

* * *

"Why does it seem like the day before vacation all hell always breaks loose in the ER?" Stanley asked, as he and Danielle boarded Flight 384 bound for Miami.

"That was a little nuts. All that salty food during Thanksgiving always loads the ER with Congestive Heart Failure Patients."

"Guess you're right. It just seemed nuttier."

"Ramona stopped by and wished us a nice vacation. She seemed a little sad even though she was smiling."

"I mentioned the interview with the Director at Fisherman's."

"Ooooh." And then Danielle continued, "When we get to the Seven Mile Bridge I want to stop at the spot where Jillena and I sprinkled Darlene's ashes over the edge."

They rented a silver Lincoln Continental at the Miami airport. Danielle had reserved a Mustang convertible, but Stanley insisted on the largest vehicle available. "Darlene told me about all the accidents that happen on A1A; humor me please."

And off they drove on the famous Overseas Highway, headed south, with plans to stop only when the road ended.

Following a leisurely drive, they pulled into a Holiday Inn at mile marker 99. "You're going to love this place!" Danielle said excitedly. "The actual African Queen from Humphrey Bogart's movie is moored here and they give dinner cruises on it!"

"You're kidding!"

"Nope. See there it is!"

That evening Stanley and Danielle enjoyed a two hour dinner cruise on the African Queen. They both felt like they were watching a dream as the little ship chugged past the palm trees in the harbor and out into the warm ocean waters.

If either Stanley or Danielle had experienced an evening of such glorious pure love, neither could recall it. The warm Gulf Stream air came in gusts, ruffling their hair and at one point blowing Stanley's favorite old Hard Rock baseball hat into the ocean. They laughed as the red cap slowly sank, and Danielle promised she would find a replacement in Key West. As the little steamboat turned back towards the distant shore, they stood in the stern, embracing, as they watched the sun set into the Atlantic Ocean. Danielle could feel Stanley's heart pounding against her when they kissed as the sun disappeared beyond the horizon.

Walking down the dock from the African Queen, Danielle said, "Tomorrow morning after breakfast, let's stop at the Dolphin Research

Center on Grassy Key. Jillena and I stopped there on the way back to Miami. I didn't know how intelligent they are."

"I'd like that. I've never seen a dolphin up close."

* * *

At mile marker 59, the silver Lincoln turned right and stopped at the Dolphin Research Center.

Stanley and Danielle walked out on the wooden dock hand in hand just in time to watch a grad student conducting IQ tests with Flipper's granddaughter.

"We're trying to ascertain dolphins' ability to comprehend numbers and to do simple math," the young man replied when queried about the activity. "We put a series of dominos in the water with a certain number of dots on each and then she swims over to the answer board and selects the domino with the sum total number of the dots."

"How's she doing?" Danielle asked.

"Funny thing," the young grad student commented, "yesterday she got every single test right. Today she's gotten every one wrong. Watch."

And Flipper's granddaughter again added the dots and gave a wrong answer.

"How can she get every one right yesterday and every one wrong today? Even if she was just guessing, she would have mixed results on both days," Stanley commented.

"Well, I think she's pissed at us today and getting every answer wrong intentionally," the young man replied.

"Why?" asked Danielle.

"We caught her with a wild male dolphin that had jumped the fence last night. She didn't want anything to do with us this morning after we escorted the young male through the gate and back into the Gulf."

"See what I mean honey, they are *way* smarter than we realize," Danielle said, looking at Stanley. "I'd be getting all the numbers wrong too!"

At the 49 mile marker they spotted it on the left side of the highway: a tan colored one story building that looked more like a fort than a hospital, except for the sign over the entrance with a jumping dolphin and FISHERMAN'S HOSPITAL in big blue letters.

"Hey man, can I help you?" asked the young man at the ER door, sporting a ponytail and a Tommy Bahama shirt.

"Hi, I'm Stanley McMillen and this is my fiancée Danielle. We're nurses from up north just stopping by to see the Director of Nursing."

"Oh, you want to see Karen. I'll call her for you, wait here. I'm Doctor Johnny Cash by the way.......no relation."

"Nice to meet you Dr. Cash. Thanks for helping."

The director appeared almost immediately. "Hi, I'm Karen. I'm so glad you two stopped by."

Stanley recognized why a bond had developed between this gray haired lady and Darlene. Karen stood about five foot, seven inches tall with an athletic figure. Through wire rim glasses, her piercing aqua blue eyes appeared to be amused, interrogating and kind. Her countenance felt welcoming as she first shook Danielle's and then Stanley's hand. She spoke softly with a southern accent.

Karen took Stanley and Danielle on a tour of the recently renovated facility.

"We're the main trauma hospital for the middle Keys," she said, "and we're very good at it. Fisherman's is now a level two trauma center. And......we can now weather a category one hurricane!"

They toured for thirty minutes, concluding in the director's office.

"I'd like it very much, Stanley and Danielle, if you came to work with us. I think with the experience you both have, we would be an even better hospital, and I know you would love working here."

"We're honored to be considered with such high esteem Karen," Danielle replied.

"Thank you," Stanley said. "Thank you for the employment opportunity. We're on our way to Key West. I promise we'll get back with you. You have a wonderful hospital and it would be an honor to work for you."

"Yes, thank you very much for your time," Danielle added.

"I'm happy you stopped by. It's wonderful to meet you after all that Darlene told me about the both of you."

"Darlene was a very special lady."

"She was a very special friend. I still think about her almost every day. I miss her laugh the most," Karen said softly.

After saying goodbye they headed south and drove up the Seven Mile Bridge. Halfway over, Danielle pointed to a No Parking sign.

"Pull over right here."

They got out of the car and walked to the Gulf side of the bridge and looked down at the light blue water.

"This is where Jillena and I stopped," Danielle said quietly.

They stood on the bridge with their arms wrapped around each other, looking down at the rhythmic waves crashing against the bridge supports for several minutes.

"We'll see her again soon enough honey," Stanley whispered.

Just then a Florida State Police patrol car pulled up with its overhead flashers on.

"You can't stop on the bridge," barked the Trooper.

"Sorry officer. We were just saying goodbye to a friend. We're leaving now," Danielle said.

"No stopping on the bridge; I'll give you a citation if you do it again."

"Yes sir, we understand."

They drove south until they reached Big Pine Key.

"There's a place called the No Name Pub on this island. Let's see if we can find it," Danielle said. "Darlene told me they make the best pizza in the Keys."

After driving around Big Pine for 30 minutes, and avoiding little Key deer standing in the road, a sign proclaimed, "YOU FOUND IT."

Following a lunch of pub pizza, it was over the bridge to Key West.

They drove slowly down Duval Street, marveling at the variety of characters wandering the sidewalks, until they reached the end. The address on the gate proclaimed, "One Duval - Pier House Resort." Room 425 was reserved in their names for the next 28 days.

The sunset at Mallory Square that evening illuminated the western sky with a spectacular slowly twisting kaleidoscope of gold, mixing with red, ending with a green flash. Gradually the crowd and nightly performers drifted away towards the Cuban bar, El Meson de Pepe, and the nocturnal Duval festivities. Stanley and Danielle stayed, sitting on the break-wall listening to the big waves crashing against the concrete.

They listened intently as Mother Ocean spoke in a language that mesmerizes all, but few understand. She told them tattletales of past lovers and great dreamers. She spoke of their accomplishments great and small, powered by love. She whispered of lasting legacies and joyous inspirations, even when tempered by tragedy, times of great fear and failure.

Eventually the crashing waves diminished to ripples... lap, lap, lapping on the worn old cement pier.

"I can hear Norma saying, 'cherish love...cherish love,'" Stanley said, looking down at the dark Atlantic illuminated by the soft glow from the street lamps. "It was the last thing she said to me."

"I hear the Beatles singing, 'Love... Love... Love...' Remember that song?"

"Sure do. I was 15."

"Then I was 7."

They embraced tightly and kissed a long impassioned kiss.

"Let's go back to our room," Danielle suggested.

"Tired?"

"Nope."

As they walked down Greene Street and turned left towards The Pier House, a band in Captain Tony's played "Unchained Melody."

"I never in my wildest dreams thought I would be in such a beautiful place with a gorgeous lady. This is wonderful."

"Yes it is, honey.....yes it is."

The next morning they ate breakfast at Blue Heaven then walked to the docks where they boarded a catamaran named Yankee Freedom for the 70 mile trip to the Dry Tortugas and Fort Jefferson. They spent the day exploring the huge old brick fort that had been used as a civil war prison, enjoyed a picnic lunch, and snorkeled around the fort until it was time to return to Key West. Once, when he turned from looking out the boat window on the way back to Key West, Stanley saw Danielle staring at him with adoration.

"I'm a little tired," Danielle commented as they stepped off the boat and headed for The Pier House, but I want us to go to the Green Parrot tonight. I read that's where the locals hang out."

* * *

It was dark as they walked down Whitehead Street towards the Green Parrot.

A sign above the front door said, NO SNIVELLING SINCE 1890.

Eleven o'clock and the crowd of partiers bulged out the doors. Every seat was taken except for a tall table next to an open window. A man in his 70's sat at the table alone, drinking a beverage from a tall glass. He had a short white beard and looked a lot like Ernest Hemmingway. Danielle and Stanley worked their way through the crowd until they arrived at the table.

"May we join you? "Stanley asked.

"If you are with this pretty lady you may," was the reply.

"I sure am. This is Danielle, my fiancée. I'm Stanley. We're two tired nurses on vacation trying to recharge our batteries."

"I'm Captain Quinn O'Malley, glad to make your acquaintance," he said as he held his hand out to Danielle.

His handsome smile revealed a missing front tooth.

"Nurses you say. Interesting work. That how you guys met?"

"Yes sir it is. May I buy you a drink?"

"You may, as long as it's Mount Gay Rum, the only thing worth drinking, I say."

"Mount Gay Rum it is, and we'll join you, right Danielle?"

"I'm sure I'd love it," Danielle stated with a smile, "but I'm drinking for two now, so I'll stick with club soda."

"With child huh?...nothing more beautiful than a lady with child." Captain O'Malley continued, "I have three kids...that I know of." He smiled. "Two daughters live in Santiago de Cuba and my youngest daughter lives in St Augustine with her mother."

"Do you get to spend time with your daughters?" Stanley asked.

"I do from time to time," replied the Captain. "And I congratulate the two of you. It's yours, right Stan?"

Danielle feigned a slap at the Captain as she laughed and said, "He's the one and only mister!" And she continued, "You look a lot like the pictures of Hemmingway that I've seen, Captain."

"Well I thank you I suppose. I did win a look-a-like contest over at Sloppy Joe's a few years back. That's about all we had in common young lady. He could write a book and I can't, and I'm alive and he ain't."

"What kind of boat do you have Captain?" Stanley asked.

"I've got a 36 foot Taylor Craft down at the marina by Conch Republic. Built in 1948 she was, and she's a beautiful lady. Her name is the Key West Dreamer. I do charter cruises for groups and such. No fishing."

"How long you been a Captain?" Stanley asked.

"Almost fifty years young man.....fifty years."

The Mount Gay Rum went down smoothly and the tall glasses were filled frequently. Danielle had one sip from Stanley's glass and smiled at the Caption with approval. She ordered club soda with a twist of lime. The bar band played cover songs loudly. Drunk and happy, the crowd swayed and danced with enthusiasm, shaking the old building as the wooden floors trembled.

"You know Captain, a number of years ago we had a doctor and his office nurse run off together. Word was they came to Key West. When his wife's private detective found them, they hired a charter captain to take them to some Caribbean island and were never heard from again."

"What was his name?" asked Captain O'Malley.

"Dr. A.W. Blue. His office nurse's name was Rita."

"Never heard of them," the Captain replied.

The festivities grew in intensity at the Green Parrot as the night progressed. Danielle and Stanley watched with astonished amusement.

About 1am, Captain Quinn O'Malley leaned over the table. Stanley and Danielle leaned in close to the Captain.

"I know which island....you want to go?"

Danielle smiled.

Stanley nodded to the affirmative.

"You kids got passports...?"

"No sir," Stanley answered over the roar of the patrons, with a questioning look.

Captain O'Malley pulled a ball-point pen from his shirt pocket and wrote on a bar napkin.

"Tomorrow I want you to walk down Petronia Street past Blue Heaven until you hit Whitehead. On the left you'll see a little brick building with a sign above the door, 'Conch Republic Passports.' Give the lady this note." And he handed the napkin to Danielle.

The writing on the napkin read, "Norah friends need passports thanks Quinn."

"She's a bit pricey, but she'll make you some good passports tomorrow. Meet me at the docks right in front of the Seafood Company, Saturday at 8am sharp."

And with that, Captain Quinn O'Malley finished his tall glass of Mount Gay Rum, lifted Danielle's right hand and kissed it gently with his sun cracked lips. "Bring enough stuff for three days," he said. Pushing his way through the crowd, the Captain disappeared into the darkness.

"He never said where we're going!" Danielle exclaimed. There was uncertain excitement in her voice.

Together they squeezed through the enthusiasm, exited beneath the dimly lit "NO SNIVELING" sign, and walked hand in hand east on Southard Street towards Duval, as the stars began to fade in the fog.

"I'm game if you are," said Stanley as they turned left on Duval, "but we will not be getting on any boat until we know where it's headed."

"When I was flying back from Alaska, I thought what an adventure life would be with you. I called that one right!" Danielle exclaimed.

Stanley squeezed her hand.

"Sometimes this girl likes being a little scared...on purpose," she said.

Chapter 31

Seldom As They Seem

S tanley glanced at his left wrist as he walked with Danielle down a deserted Greene Street past Sloppy Joe's towards the marina. The hands on his Nautica watch pointed to 8:23. A gusty south breeze stirred the sticky tropical air and blew Danielle's curly auburn hair in all directions. The gutters on either side of the street smelled of urine, and Danielle gagged several times as they walked along.

"Morning sickness?"

"Nope....just never been a fan of stale urine in the morning," Danielle laughed.

"That was fun at Schooner Wharf last night," Stanley commented as they strolled towards the marina. "I think their rubbed wings are the best wings I've ever eaten."

"I love sitting outside with the band playing and the dogs wandering around begging for treats...and beer," Danielle said with a smile. "I love dogs.

"Those were some interesting stories the bartender told us last night about Quinn O'Malley," Danielle continued.

"Weren't they!" Stanley exclaimed. "I would never have guessed, looking at him now, that he studied law at the University of Havana."

"And that he was a classmate of Fidel Castro's in 1947. Wonder if they're friends?" Danielle replied.

"That off-duty cop sitting on the barstool next to you was an interesting character too!"

"Wasn't he? I think he was trying to pick me up until I flashed my ring... repeatedly," Danielle laughed.

"Can't fault his taste in ladies," Stanley said with a grin. "And when you asked him about Captain O'Malley, he winked and told you, 'He's an upstanding citizen,' as he lit that Bolivar cigar from Habana."

"That story about Captain O'Malley and a friend running the Cuban embargo, and eluding the naval blockade in the 60's with contraband sounded like a scene from a movie. He has had an adventurous life," Danielle said.

"I really think that bartender was the 'friend' on the boat with O'Malley," Stanley said. "The flares in the night sky... being chased by a Navy Destroyer and hit by machine gun fire before out-running the Navy while Air Force jets flew over looking for them in the dark. Then, the Cuban Navy escorting them into Havana harbor. Yup, he had to be that 'friend' with O'Malley.

"You still ok going with him?"

"We'll see...," Danielle replied.

* * *

They could hear the slow throb of the Key West Dreamer's twin 200 horse power engines as they approached the marina in front of the Conch Republic Sea Food Company

Captain O'Malley was sitting in a folding beach chair on the cruiser's deck, smoking a pipe. When he spotted the approaching couple, he looked at his watch and then pointed at the time.

"Sorry Captain," Stanley apologized, as he nodded towards Danielle and winked.

"Well, we have 200 miles ahead of us; it'll take us all night with these seas. Welcome aboard. You kids have your passports?"

Stanley produced two U.S passports, blue in color with gold print and emblem on the cover.

"How did that Norah lady get our passports so quickly?" Stanley asked. "She had them for us Thursday."

"I doubt they're legal, Captain… she didn't even ask for our birth certificates," Danielle added, with a hint of sarcasm.

"Norah has friends in high places. Do they look legal?"

"Yup," Stanley and Danielle replied.

"There you go!"

"How much is this trip going to cost us, Captain? Didn't have a chance to ask the other night at the Parrot."

"What trip?" Captain O'Malley retorted as he stood up.

"I have one rather important question for you, Captain," Danielle said as she touched his arm.

"Yes?"

"Just where are we going?"

Captain O'Malley took the pipe from his mouth and laughed loudly.

"Cayo Coco!"

"Where?" Stanley inquired.

"Barrier Island off the north coast of Cuba; best beaches in the Caribbean."

"That's illegal!" Danielle exclaimed.

"Not to worry young lady. I have many friends in high places, never had a problem, and neither will you guys. I promise you this."

"I've wanted to go to Cuba since I was a kid!" Stanley exclaimed. "LET'S GO!"

"LET'S!" Danielle agreed. "I love an adventure…always have!"

And she gave Stan a nudge.

A dock hand freed the lines from the mooring posts, and the white, wooden-hulled cruiser with African mahogany and teak decking, slowly left the marina and rounded Tank Island to the starboard and then headed south-southeast at 10 knots.

Danielle and Stanley stood on the deck watching Mallory Square fade in the morning fog. When the mainland had disappeared, Danielle moved closer to Stanley, placed both arms around his neck and pulled his face close to hers.

"You make me laugh more than anyone else I have known. My life has become an adventure with you. You make my heart smile. I love this!"

* * *

A pink eastern sky announced the arrival of Sunday morning. The sun peeked over the silhouette of Cuba as the Key West Dreamer approached the Cayo Coco marina.

Without warning, a spotlight at the entrance to the marina flicked on, the brilliant white light searching the dark rolling waves, finally stopping on the approaching cruiser. Captain O'Malley maneuvered directly towards the light. Behind the spotlight stood a tall uniformed man with a submachine gun slung over his shoulder.

"Hola Raul, veo que estas trabajando el primer turno de la manana," Captain O'Malley said to a man standing at the entrance to the marina.

"Buenos dias Captain O'Malley. Estoy muy feliz de verte otra vez."

"Tengo dos queridos amigos que quieren disfrutar de su hospitalidad. Son amigos del Dr. Blue," Captain O'Malley answered.

"Cualquier amigo del Dr. Blue es bienvenido aqui!" the guard answered.

"Damn...I wish I understood Spanish," Stanley whispered to Danielle.

"No kidding. At least he looks happy!"

Captain O'Malley threw the guard a bow line, who secured it to a post.

Then the captain went below, returning with a blue bank deposit pouch. He handed it to the man he called Raul.

"Muchas gracias," the guard said. He took the deposit pouch to the guard-house, and returned with two large brown canvas satchels.

"Monte Christos and Bolivars!" the guard said as he handed the lumpy bags to Captain Quinn.

Captain O'Malley winked as he reached into one of the satchels and handed Stanley a wooden cigar box stamped MONTECRISTO Habana, Cuba.

"I am just a simple International Ambassador," Quinn O'Malley said as he smiled at Danielle. "These cigars will be smoked in Washington D.C. next month."

Stanley and Danielle stepped off the boat and entered Cuba. Stanley handed the guard both passports. He opened them briefly before smiling and welcoming them to his country. "Aprobado. Bienvenido a Cuba!"

Stanley turned back and faced the Key West Dreamer.

"You've been approved," Captain O'Malley said with a wry smile.

"At least let me give you something to help with the fuel costs, Captain."

The two men stared at each other for several seconds as the boat bobbed about. And then Captain O'Malley motioned with his right hand for Stanley and Danielle to bend close to him.

"You guys bought the Mount Gay at the Parrot ...let's call it even."

He paused.

"...and you both befriended a lonely old alcoholic captain, and trusted him. That is payment enough."

Danielle stepped back on the boat. She placed both hands on either side of the captain's gray whiskered face. Pulling his face close to her, she gently kissed him on the forehead as she said, "It is our honor to make your friendship Quinn O'Malley," and then she rejoined Stanley on the dock.

Captain O'Malley wiped several tears from his weathered face with the back of his left hand. He handed Stanley a 3 by 5 card with a phone number scribbled on it.

"I'll be back on Thursday. Be at this dock at 8am sharp." And he winked at Danielle. "Call that number if you need a ride sooner!" he shouted as he put the idling boat in reverse. The guard threw the bow line onto the Key West Dreamer's deck as the cruiser slowly turned and then headed north-northwest.

"Captain made arrangements... Hotel Blau Colonial," Raul said in broken English as he hailed a cab on his radio. Soon a 1958 Ford station wagon arrived.

Stanley handed Raul a twenty dollar bill as they put two carry-on bags into the back of the old car.

"Muchas gracias amigo," Raul said with a smile.

"It reminds me of the Don Cesar in St Pete," Danielle exclaimed as they drove up the drive towards the large pink Spanish colonial hotel. "It's the same pink color."

Stanley and Danielle were exhausted after a night battling 6 foot waves. After a much needed 7 hour nap and a refreshing shower, they headed for the beach to watch the sunset.

The tide trickled in as they approached an old man sitting alone in a wooden beach chair, bathing his bare feet in the warm Atlantic saltwater. His long white hair dangled over the back of the chair as he stared out at the ocean. The chair next to him sat empty.

Danielle's laughter startled the old man. He jerked and turned his head and peered intently in the sunset light. An opaque ring of Arcus Senilis circled the periphery of his brown eyes, which suddenly flashed with recognition.

"Stanley?!"

"A.W.! It's the long haired version of you!" Stanley exclaimed as he leaned down and shook the old man's hand.

"What the hell are you doing here, Stanley?"

"We were in the neighborhood and thought we'd stop by and say hi," Stanley replied, with a big grin on his face.

"Actually, Dr. Blue, Captain O'Malley brought us here," Danielle chimed in.

"He's a good man ...O'Malley. He never charged Rita and me a cent. He's a cigar runner you know."

"We know now!" Danielle replied.

"Dr. Blue, I'm pleased to introduce you to my fiancée, Danielle."

"I'm happy to meet you Danielle. You must be a special lady to put up with the likes of this character. Did he ever tell you the goldfish story?"

"No sir."

"Well. Here is the type of bastard you are betrothed to. I had an inguinal hernia repair....are you a nurse?"

"That's how we met," Danielle responded with a wink.

"Good...well, I came out of surgery and was shaking off the anesthetic. I looked up at the IV bottles and one of them had a goldfish swimming around and around. I thought I was hallucinating, so I closed my eyes. Two hours later that damn little fish was still swimming around. I was afraid to say anything to the attending staff, but finally called for Stanley. He said, 'You see *what*, Doc? Want a little scotch?' And then he laughed so hard I thought he was going to pee his pants. He had put a goldfish in a bottle of normal saline and made it look like it was attached to my intravenous lines. Damn him!"

Danielle laughed, caught her breath and laughed again.

"I've got a few stories too!" Danielle replied.

"Well, as long as you know what you're getting into my dear."

Dr. Blue paused, and then with his voice barely auditable over the sound of the waves, continued, "I imagine they are all gone now, the staff and people who would remember me. What about Chief, Stan... I was afraid of Chief. She was always right. At least I learned to listen to her." He chuckled. "I imagine she is long since retired, huh?"

"She died a few months ago, A.W.; died from lung cancer. She's buried next to the Chief of Police Johnson on the bluffs overlooking the bay."

Dr. Blue smiled and asked, "Did they ever get married?"

"You knew about them?"

"Charlie Johnson and I were great friends, Stan."

"Nope, they were never married."

Danielle plopped down in the empty chair.

"Where's Rita, A.W.?" Stanley asked, as he pulled a third heavy chair through the white sand, and then sat down facing Dr. Blue.

Pointing with an arthritic right index finger towards the setting sun, he replied, "Out there. She's out there. Rita died from breast cancer three years ago and I sprinkled her out there."

"I'm sorry," Danielle and Stanley uttered in unison.

"She was a good friend. I come here most evenings and listen. Rita whispers things to me from the waves."

There was a pause that lasted several minutes.

"Danielle and Stanley I want you to listen to me very closely now." The old man took a deep breath.

"I was the almighty A.W. Blue, former Chief of Staff at Big Bay General, and the Surgical Section Chief. I was impressed that I was really something special and I believed it. It was all about me all of those years. I had no time left over for my wife; Carole eventually found the appreciation and affections she deserved with the guys over at the Coast Guard base."

Dr. Blue took another deep breath.

"It was my own damn fault. I left town when I discovered her Coast Guard affairs. It was the least I could do for her, keep the spotlight on me and reap the wrath. It was a hard lesson to learn, that love is really not all about me."

The rising warm salty water now lapped at their knees.

"The people in town were shocked and some of the hospital staff was mad as hell over what you did A.W.," Stanley commented.

"Good…it worked. What became of Carole?"

"She married a pilot a few years later. They moved to Florida when he was transferred to Air Station Clearwater."

Dr. Blue smiled.

"You two want to work with me?" Dr. Blue asked.

"What do you mean?" Danielle asked.

"I have a clinic in the basement of The Colonial; see rich Europeans, mostly Germans on vacation, and some Canadians. Treat social diseases, colds, flu and hangovers…..nothing serious."

"We're so honored to be asked," Danielle replied. "We have a lot to consider in our lives, and we'll add that to our list." And she reached over and squeezed the doctor's hand.

"Yes we will," Stanley added. "Thanks A.W."

"Think about it. This is a wonderful place to live."

Dr. Blue continued, "And when those days come, the days when your mind is all puffed up and you feel full of yourself, remember my disappointing story. If you love each other absolutely, you'll both be number one. Remember that from an old man who now knows."

"Yes sir."

"No conditions…none! Conditional love is an oxymoron," Dr. Blue continued.

"Thank you for sharing with us A.W."

At that moment a rogue wave interrupted the conversation, almost upending Danielle as the water rushed over her at chin level.

She laughed as she struggled to her feet, spitting out a salty mouthful.

The three Americans waded to the new water line and then walked down the white beach towards the dimly illuminated pink hotel.

"I'm glad you found me," said Dr. Blue as they walked together. He shook Stanley's hand, hugged Danielle and turned and walked away, disappearing on the darkening beach.

"Isn't it something?" Danielle commented, as they walked into the hotel lobby. "Things are seldom as they seem."

"Ain't that the truth!"

Fifteen minutes later Danielle walked out of the shower with just a towel wrapped around her head. She flopped on the bed, belly up.

"My belly itches, would you rub some lotion on it please…?"

Stanley filled his left hand with rose scented lotion and softly rubbed her belly in a circular fashion.

"I want to go back to Big Bay when our vacation is over," Danielle whispered, with her eyes closed, "and live there. Let's get married and raise our baby there. I really don't want to move anywhere. I love that town Stanley."

"I do too! Every time I return from a conference or vacation, and drive through downtown, I think how lucky we are to live in such a beautiful place, with truly kind people who care about each other.

"I sure am in love with you," Stanley continued. "Maybe we should ask Captain O'Malley to marry us?"

"Can he?"

"He's a licensed sea captain. I remember reading an article once that said something like, 'The Master of the vessel may officiate at a marriage on that vessel.' The catch is, the vessel must be in international waters. When we get back to Key West, let's go down to the courthouse and get a marriage license!"

"Let's! He would be so honored and we can honeymoon in Key West. We have room 425 until the end of December."

Danielle opened her hazel eyes and stared at her lover.

"I've searched for you for as long as I can remember. You're my best friend and I want us to be together forever."

"Forever... I promise."

Five minutes later Danielle was sound asleep.

Stanley reached up and turned the bedside lamp off, allowing a soft blue light from a nearly full moon to flood the room through the balcony windows.

Lying next to the love that had changed his life, Stanley listened to her soft breathing. A rush of trembling warmth flashed over his body as he gently moved closer and whispered, "Thank you Jesus," in her ear.

A smile flickered on her lips between slumbering breaths.

At that moment, Stanley knew he could abandon any earthly thing for this love.

EPILOG

"I wonder how many people I've looked at all my life and never seen."

John Steinbeck

To be continued…

Richard Alan Hall
lives in Traverse City,
Michigan with
his wife Debra.